I0731787

# STARVATION

Molly Fennig

Immortal Works LLC
1505 Glenrose Drive
Salt Lake City, Utah 84104
Tel: (385) 202-0116

© 2020 Molly Fennig
http://mollyfennig.com/

Cover Art by Ashley Literski
http://strangedevotion.wixsite.com/strangedesigns

All rights reserved, including the right to reproduce this book or portions thereof in any form whatsoever. For more information email contact@immortal-works.com or visit http://www.immortal-works.com/contact/.

This book is a work of fiction. Names, characters, businesses, organizations, places, events and incidents either are the product of the author's imagination or are used fictitiously. Any resemblance to actual persons, living or dead, events, or locales is entirely coincidental.

ISBN 978-1-953491-99-2 (Paperback)
ASIN B08LB64P1Q (Kindle Edition)

*To Bella*
*and the Molly who inspired this book.*

## AUTHOR'S NOTE

**Trigger warning**: This book covers difficult topics such as eating disorders, suicide, and depression.

This story is not meant to represent all eating disorder stories, nor everyone who experiences them. Further, I hope that I have not glorified these diseases in any way, nor vilified those who suffer from them. My goal is to bring awareness to an often-ignored area, namely men who struggle with eating disorders and suicidality. Hopefully, this awareness will help decrease the stigma of mental illness and start much-needed conversations.

If reading this book brings up difficult feelings (anxiety, despair, eating disorder symptoms, etc.) please reach out to someone. I have included a few resources below that I hope are helpful.

*You matter. What you feel is valid. And just because you feel something (like hopeless) does not mean your situation is.*

National Eating Disorders Association (NEDA) Helpline: (800) 931-2237
www.nationaleatingdisorders.org

National Suicide Prevention Hotline: 1-800-273-8255
   https://suicidepreventionlifeline.org/

For mental health information, support groups, and more visit https://nami.org.

To find a mental health provider in your area, covered by your insurance, go to https://www.psychologytoday.com/us/therapists.

# 1
# AFTER

I should have been dead, but that was the kind of thing my family never talked about. Mom had fallen asleep in the chair by my hospital bed, dried mascara caked under her eyes. Dad had gone off to get coffee, or so he said, but I think he was tired of looking anywhere but at me. Collin hadn't even come. Not that we'd been talking much since the car accident and his new girlfriend and junior year in general. We'd only been friends since kindergarten. No big deal.

The hospital wristband cuts at the bones protruding from my wrist. *Wes McCoy*, it labels me, but they haven't put *crazy* or *stupid* or *fat*, so I know the label is not quite complete.

I slip the hospital wrist band on and off because there is nothing else to do besides count ceiling tiles, which I've already done for one hundred and thirty-three minutes straight.

An elderly lady with a puff of white hair and crooked glasses shuffles by the sliding glass door, the bottom of her walker covered in tennis balls. I close my eyes and wonder how things would be different if I had been a tennis player instead of a wrestler.

EARLIER THAT DAY we had practice with lift and conditioning afterwards. I rushed to the locker room after US Government, a mere hour early, to change. Checked every row. Found no one. Threw on a T-shirt, shorts and sweats, even though the school was cranked up to eighty degrees to overcompensate for the December frost.

My stomach growled. I pulled out a smashed granola bar from my pocket. I closed my eyes and imagined crispy chicken, green beans drenched in butter, chocolate ice cream, and cherries, and threw the bar in the bottom of my locker. I downed an entire bottle of water to make everything stop spinning as much, even though all I wanted to do was grab the granola bar and shove the entire thing in my mouth.

Ten minutes into practice, I was dripping sweat, my heartbeat erratic, everything gaining a slight blur. I didn't take off the sweats, though, needing to lose the water weight. Needing to move down another weight class to have a better chance at being more like Jason.

Collin didn't say anything to me, laughing with Alex during water breaks and talking with Jackson on the way back. During one and two-foot takedowns, Collin had me on the mat in less than a second, over and over, while I had to throw myself at him to get him down once.

I lay on the mat as darkness pressed at the sides of my vision. My head floated in waves. Collin ran a hand though his dirty-blond hair, rolling his eyes. "You going to get up, McCoy?"

Instead of kicking his feet out from under him, which in hindsight, maybe I should have, I stood up. The darkness pulsed, and the floor rose back up to catch me. When I opened my eyes, the entire wrestling team and two paramedics stared from above. I was sure this was how I was going to die—on the sweaty wrestling room floor, shivering so hard my muscles stabbed with pain, my chest exploding, my vision blurry.

Dr. Allen opens the sliding glass door. "How are you feeling?"

Mom's eyes flutter open and she leans forward, reaching for my hand. I pull it away, letting her hand fall on my thigh.

"Uh, okay I guess." I slip the hospital band off and back on.

"What's wrong? Is it serious?" Mom's grip on me has tightened, her left foot bouncing.

"Actually, I wanted to talk to you outside first, if that's alright."

The fidgeting increases but she follows him. His shoulders are straight, head high, but he betrays this confidence by adjusting the stethoscope around his neck, pointing to the chart. They both look at me. Mom's face sinks, her head shaking back and forth. He puts his hand on her shoulder, assuring her he is right. She cups her face with her hands, body shaking with sobs.

I slide the wristband off. Back on. Off. Back on.

Dad steps in, carrying a cup of coffee that he places on the nurse's stand before taking Mom in his arms. He looks at Dr. Allen to explain. He looks at me the same way—as if I had sprouted an extra arm—before burying his face in Mom's hair.

I slide the wristband off. Back on. Off. Back on.

The sliding door creeps open. Mom and Dad huddle in the corner. Dr. Allen sits down in a chair, which I know is an attempt to get me to feel more "comfortable" with "being vulnerable" and "sharing." I cross my arms.

"When is the last time you ate, Wes?" he asks, eyes landing on the clipboard, finding his perception of me.

I wonder if this means they think I need surgery or had an allergic reaction, which I hope for, instead of them knowing the real reason I fainted and the real reason I can't be here any longer.

# 2
# BEFORE

It was 8:00 am, a year ago, when I was a sophomore, and if Jason had remarked one more time about how beautiful the sunset was or how excited he was for this tournament, I would have thrown him out of the old, red Honda minivan, even though traffic by the high school was almost stopped. I covered my face with a Hayfield High sweatshirt as Jason sipped his Caribou coffee and smiled at the snowflakes sticking to the windshield. I set my phone on top of my cooler filled with blue Gatorade and PowerBars, sandwiches, nuts, cheese, and bananas for the day. I hated waiting until after weigh-ins for breakfast.

Dad turned up the volume on *Yellow Submarine*. It did nothing to muffle his less-than-generous comments about the other Minnesota drivers, though. He pulled up to let us off at the entrance, thanks to the semi-blizzard.

"Dad, unlock the doors." I pulled my duffel bag onto my lap, hand on the door handle.

"Not before I say what I have to say."

"McCoys were born to be wrestlers. Blah blah. I think we got it." I tugged. Still locked.

"Wes, let the man speak. He knows what he's talking about." Jason cocked his head intently, as if he hadn't heard this speech forty-thousand times, too.

I sunk into my seat, hand pressed to the frosted window.

"You, my sons, are the next of the McCoy wrestlers, descendants of Grandpa McCoy, the first Hayfield High wrestler to make it to state. And Uncle Jim and myself, All-State for three years, State

Champs for two. Now, Jason, my eldest, already All-State as a freshman and State Champ the two years after. And Wes, now a sophomore that no one is going to see coming. Have fun. Make us proud."

I pulled on the door. I hated how my name sounded, with no awards and the fact that the only good thing about me was that no one expected anything. The lock clicked, and I barreled out into the snow, loving the sharp sting of the cold air, how it numbed everything.

Kids clumped around cafeteria tables that overflowed with blankets, jackets, bags, and food that various parents had felt obligated to contribute. I spotted a blotch of gold and sat down next to Andre, who had just cut his afro so now the black curls were almost subdued. Next to him was Nate who always looked like he should have a tan, salmon shorts, and a cheap warm beer instead of a gold-and-black spandex singlet.

"Hey." We mutually head-nodded, all of us too cool to engage in small talk.

Jason came up behind me, putting his arm around my shoulder, grinding a knuckle in my hair until I wiggled away. "Good luck, bro."

My face burned, even though Nate and Andre were too busy worshipping my older brother to notice me.

Kathryn Douglas already sat at the head of the table. She was petite and soft with straightened-to-death blonde hair and a permanently fake smile. She attacked Jason with a kiss before he even set his bag down.

"Hey, babe." He tucked a piece of hair behind her ear. "Thanks for coming."

"You know I wouldn't miss it."

I tried not to gag as I searched for my water bottle, going off to find a fountain even though the bottle was already full. I passed two girls, arms interlaced as they whispered to each other, covered completely in pink. Ballet shoes and tights and tutus and leotards and ribbons, all the same light pink as the pale streaks in the pre-sunrise sky.

Underneath my sweatshirt, I pulled at my wrestling uniform, the straps hanging near my waist, hating how the spandex clung so tightly to the fat and muscle-less-ness and everything else. The girls looked through me, laughing as if I wasn't there. I took a left, then two rights before I found a fountain. I dumped out my water and refilled it.

When I got back, Collin had arrived. He was only ten minutes late this time, and had actually combed his blond hair. "Yo, McCoy."

"Hey Anderson. Nice of you to make it." I glanced over. Jason paced up and down the hall instead of taking his usual pre-match nap, resting his head on the cafeteria table, a balled-up jacket as a pillow. Kathryn placed a hand on his shoulder and he brushed it off.

Collin peeled off his sweatshirt. "You know, I have to give the fans what they want."

I snorted, even with my attention on Jason. Alex head-nodded as he passed. Jason lifted his chin, but without a Jasonian "hey man" or "what's up?"

Collin punched me on the shoulder. "My greatness is no joke, McCoy."

"Whatever you say, Anderson." I laughed.

At the end of the day, Collin came in third in his weight class, the one below mine. I came in second. And Jason, of course, took first. I took his picture with Dad, the trophy in between them, which we sent to Mom. A crisis with a design client had come up, something about the drapes being too "eggplant," whatever that meant.

Collin held up his third-place medal kissing his biceps and pretending to encourage the roar of his adoring fans. I shook my head and went to fill my water bottle for the half-hour drive home, finishing off another PowerBar on my way.

A girl sat on the windowsill in the hallway, looking out as if she were in a sad movie. She had the entire pink ensemble, too, but instead of a tight, blonde bun, she had a fiery cloud. I only got a few steps before she raised her head, catching my eyes with hers, tear-stained and mascara-smeared.

I gave a sympathetic smile, but she didn't break eye contact.

"Are you okay?"

"Yeah." She wiped her eyes with the sleeve of her leotard. "Thanks."

I took my gaze off her, off her sad, hazel eyes brimming with storm clouds, the freckles scattered over her cheeks like stars, to watch the water gush jerkily from the spout.

"You wrestle." There was no question to it, just the hitch of a voice previously inundated by tears.

"Yeah. You dance?" Mine was a question, vibrating with the uncertainty of what to say to a strange ballerina sobbing on the windowsill of a sub-par high school.

"Ballet. We just had our recital." The storm in her eyes was passing, the weather clearing. Straight white teeth peeked out from lips bending softly upwards. "I'm Caila, by the way, Caila Brennan."

"Wes McCoy." I screwed the top back on my water bottle.

"Well, sorry you had to find me like this, but thanks." The smile solidified, sparkling in her eyes as she stood.

"For what?" I asked as she made her way further down the hall.

She said nothing, just turned around, smiled, and kept going.

And that was the day I met Caila, wondering since then how different my life would have been if I hadn't gone to the water fountain. How different my parents' and hers would have been. Maybe it wouldn't have mattered. But forgive me, I'm getting ahead of myself.

# 3
# AFTER

A younger nurse, short, with dark skin and a permanent smile, wheels me out of the hospital to the van where my parents are waiting. He gives me a few packets of instant applesauce and a box of noodles, my dinner, and tells my parents to make me eat both, at least. Enough to tamp down the hunger I am so used to but not enough to anger my stomach into forcing out what they had forced in.

The car weaves its way down Carolina Street, past the Craftsman house with white trim and a gray roof that would've looked better in black. Past the one-story rambler, its red shutters almost hidden behind the large plants in the window boxes.

I close my eyes because I know this street, these houses. I imagine knocking down the crooked bungalow and replacing it with a large house, four stories including the basement, sucking up all the empty space between it and its neighbors. Five bedrooms. Four bathrooms. Large kitchen full of food. Two ovens, one always baking cookies, the scent wafting through the house.

The van lurches to a halt, jerking my eyes open. Mom and Dad find me in the rearview mirror. I feel their gaze, the heaviness of the words left unsaid, even as we get out of the car, walk down the cracked driveway, and open the door to the dirt-colored split level we call home.

Dad puts a pot on the stained stovetop to boil water for dinner. His eyes leap from the water, to me, and back until I push away from the table, run up the stairs, and flop on my bed. My feet hang off the end like they always do unless I curl my knees up to my chest, hugging them. The walls are still a sad gray, cracks reaching down from the ceiling like fingertips toward the peeling laminate floors, the bedspread decorated with mouse-chewed holes, and nothing else, because there isn't room for more than a bed. I press my back up against the wall with the small window, closing my eyes and pretending its Jason right behind me and that the wind outside is really his breath and that my heartbeat is his, too.

I try not to go into his room since he left because there is too much I don't want to see. The Jason-shaped indent in the unmade twin bed. The piles of shorts and uniforms, gold and black for our school colors, underneath newspaper magazines. *J. McCoy Advances in Wrestling Tournament. J. McCoy Wins State. J. McCoy Carries on Family Legacy.*

"Dinner!" Mom calls. I close the door partially and descend the stairs.

The table is crammed into the corner of the kitchen that still has four chairs when we all know it should only have three. The only sounds are of the scraping of the metal spoon in the pot as Dad scoops the noodles into three red-rimmed bowls, and the screeching of my chair as I pull it out. Mom and Dad look at each other, gesturing with their eyes toward me as they sit on either side, Dad placing the bowl carefully in front of me.

I pick up the fork, turning it over in my hands, looking at the way the second tine bends to the right. I spear a noodle as I exhale, making it a motion, a command, rather than a thought. Spear noodle. Lift noodle. Open mouth. Put fork in mouth. Close and pull. Chew. Swallow. I can't. *You can do this.* Swallow. *Come on, Wes. It's this or through a nose tube.*

Mom lets out a breath and Dad takes a bite of his dinner. What a relief that I know how to eat. I take a big swig of water and bite my lip. Don't cry. You're okay. You're okay. But I can't breathe and my chest feels size double-zero tight and the room is spinning and my heart is beating so fast it might explode and Mom and Dad are still staring at me and my throat's constricting and blocking the air and I can't breathe and I'm going to die.

I manage to shove a few more bites in before I feel nauseous. I say nothing, leaving my plate on the table. It takes me five minutes to get up the stairs, my limbs so weak and on fire, my chest burning, joints aching. I get into bed, pulling four blankets on top of me, but still the cold penetrates. My skin itches, but every time I scratch it, large flakes of skin fall off. When I scratch my scalp, clumps of dead, straw-like hair come with.

Like most nights, I don't sleep much, even with three forkfuls of noodles and two of applesauce in my stomach. All I can think about is how many calories that was and how many more I will have to eat tomorrow. How much I want to eat chocolate cake with rich chocolate frosting and pork ribs drenched in barbeque sauce that fall off the bone.

But as much as I want the flavors in my mouth, my heart stops and my breath catches just thinking about having to swallow. Ten minutes pass. I turn over. Half an hour. I curl my legs up beneath me. An hour. I turn over again. An hour and a half. I stretch out like a starfish. Two hours. I grab the takeout menus tucked under my mattress and read through them, over and over.

I go to the bathroom to give my mind something to do besides think. I wonder how far I'd have to push my finger down my throat this time to make my stomach full of zero forkfuls. I stand in front of the mirror. Tell myself not to. Remind myself it will do nothing. Feel my hands reaching up, as much as I don't want them to. Close my eyes and beg myself not to do this. Open my eyes and see the skeleton staring back at me. There is nothing glamorous or beautiful about bones. *Just five more pounds and you'll be happy*, something inside me says. *This time, I promise.* It doesn't matter what the voice says, though, because my body has already decided for me. It won't listen to me as I watch it. Like the kid in the horror movie going to the basement alone, all I can do is watch and tell them to stop, to not be so stupid. And yet, the kid goes down the dark stairs. Screams. And my cracked, yellow fingertip covered in swollen scabs reaches down my throat. I try to pull it back, but my stomach is convulsing, heaving, cutting off air, and the bile is already trickling in bursts into the toilet.

# 4
# BEFORE

**M**om had dinner ready when we got back from the tournament. Succulent chicken and butter-soaked green beans and sourdough rolls. Jason and I elbowed each other as we raced up the stairs, stripping off uniforms while reaching for the bathroom door. There was barely enough hot water for one shower, especially in the winter. He had a foot out, but I blocked him by spreading my arms in the doorway. I leaned forward to dive in, but he kneed the back of my leg, sending me sprawling as he slammed and locked the door. The water gushed, and Jason began a painfully off-key, but full-volume, rendition of "Brown-eyed Girl."

I retreated to my room and turned on my laptop. *10 notifications*, all tagging me in the article about Jason winning the tournament. My cursor hovered over the X when another popped up. *Instagram follow request from Caila Brennan.*

I clicked on her profile. In her picture, she was spinning in a white dress that spun and rose with her, the background black, as rain fell and drops formed on the camera lens, the only color in the photo was from loose, fiery curls that floated behind her.

The first post was a Minnesota Dance Academy video. A large dark stage held a lone girl curled up at the center. Then, the music started. Slow and melancholy, building, like the realization of permanence. Of death, of lost love. Caila unfolded in graceful arcs, rising. Her movements became more powerful, assured, as the melody quickened and intensified. My skin tingled with goosebumps, but I didn't even notice until the video ended, and I blinked.

I followed her back before I could overthink it.

Jason ran out of songs and hot water, and I showered, shivering as the icy stream hit my back and frost formed on the window. Together we ran downstairs. We stuffed rolls in our mouths faster than we could swallow, just so we could get seconds and thirds before the other ate everything.

"Oh, I got into Stanford," Jason said between bites of green beans.

"That's great, honey!" Mom said. She and Dad made eye contact and their expressions fell.

"Don't worry, it's a full ride." Jason took a sip of water which I knew was his way to keep from saying anything else.

"Are you kidding, J? That's insane!" I yelled.

Mom dropped her fork and pulled him into a long hug. "Good for you. That's amazing!"

Dad almost knocked over his chair as he stood, embracing both of them. "So proud of you, son. So, so proud."

As they sat down, Dad's face flushed with a smile and Mom kept squeezing Jason's hand.

I grabbed a roll from the center, but Jason grabbed the other side, trying to pry it from me. I pulled it back, but he retaliated by grabbing another and pelting me on the forehead with it.

"Hey, hey, whoa." Mom picked up the platter in the center, holding it away from us. "Can we at least pretend to be civilized? I mean, this is a Stanford scholarship winning family."

Jason swallowed, then grinned. "Sorry Mom, it just takes so much to be this good."

I elbowed him, chewing my last bite of chicken.

"So, I guess Wes has no excuse," Dad joked.

I coughed—the dry, half-chewed chunks stuck in my throat. Jason hit my back and Mom set the platter back down, giving Dad the same look she had just given us.

"May I be excused?" I muttered, not waiting for a reply before retreating to my room, two steps at a time.

"Really, Josh?" Mom's words floated after me. No footsteps followed me, though, just the screech of silverware against plates.

Collin came over later, even though I texted him not to bother. "Hey, McCoy."

"Hey, Anderson." I looked up from my sketchpad. I finished the last of the skyscrapers, shaped like roses, the bottoms smaller, the tops covered in petal-like sheets of steel that swelled out, with square cutouts for windows. I loved the idea of unnatural nature, of delicate strength, of a building I could see dancing in the wind like a lone dancer on a darkened stage.

"What are we doing tonight? Feeling sorry for ourselves? Muffled sobbing?" Collin sat down next to me.

I hit him with my sketchpad. "Jason got into Stanford. Full ride for wrestling."

"Whoa. I don't see why this makes us sad, though." Collin took the drawings from me. "Because he's good at wrestling? I'd like to see him try to draw half of what you do."

I smiled, loving how Collin always said "we" and "us" and exactly the right thing, even if flower skyscrapers wouldn't get me into Stanford, free or otherwise.

"Did you bring *Starvation*?" I tucked my sketchpad into the top drawer of my nightstand, grabbing my controllers.

"Obviously. *Starvation* is the game superior to all others and, I, for one, will not let us waste time on anything but the finest pleasures in life."

I rolled my eyes. "Says the man who eats boxed macaroni and cheese every night."

"Four-hundred and thirty-seven days straight. Like I said, McCoy, only the finest pleasures."

We were on a new world, so I keep getting eaten by zombies because I was too busy observing the buildings and the skylines. Collin jumped and twisted next to me, as if it would make his character react faster. He barely looked at the buildings but made us take the time to read each piece of dialogue. *Starvation* was supposed to be set in old England, so it had lots of big words, some of which Collin wrote down on the notes page on his phone to be later incorporated into his vocabulary.

We played until Mom came in and asked what Collin's curfew was, even though Collin had been coming over for years and she knew it was 11:00. As he put on his coat he nodded at Mom. "Thank you, Mrs. McCoy, for letting me fraternize with your delightful son. I regret that I must be getting home."

"Good night, Collin." My mom laughed.

"See you at school, Anderson," I called after him.

# 5
# AFTER

Fortunately, Winter Break means no school, and being released from the hospital means no wrestling practice, even though I'm sure Mom wouldn't let me go back yet anyway. It also means I don't need to deal with the "are you okay?"s and "how are you feeling?"s and "what happened?"s from the wrestling team. Unfortunately, it also means three meals a day of extreme scrutiny, where each bite is met with a sigh of relief. From Mom and Dad, at least.

"Morning," Dad says, not looking up from the paper when I finally roll out of bed and trudge downstairs. I try not to wheeze as I collapse into the chair.

"I made pancakes. With chocolate chips," Mom says. She doesn't say that she knows they're my favorite. That she made them because she is feeling guilty and helpless and other emotions too abstract to be directly confronted.

I don't say that the pancakes are ninety-three calories, the pre-applied syrup adding another fifty-three. More than I used to eat some days, the ones where I had to drink around a gallon of water so the pain in my stomach and the emptiness hurt just enough less that I could sit up.

I take two bites, forcing them down with swigs of black coffee when they get stuck in my throat. Mom puts down her fork. "How are you feeling?"

"Okay." I draw my mouth into a smile as proof, but I want my lips to form the right words, the real words, instead.

"How did you sleep?" She wraps her hands around her coffee mug. The steam drifts upwards, curling and twisting, lost.

"Okay," I say again. Another lie. I take another bite of pancakes even though my stomach clenches and I feel sick and I might throw up and I can't breathe, can't breathe. I try to hold the bites in my mouth as long as possible, try to ingrain the feeling of the melted chocolate and sweet syrup on my tongue so I can revisit it when the hunger gets too intense or when I can't sleep or when I can't feel my fingers because they're too cold. I hold the pancakes in my mouth, too, so I can delay the inevitable panic as it slithers down my throat.

Mom interrupts my thoughts and I cough, almost choking. "I scheduled therapy for Thursday. And we should go over the new house rules."

"House rules?" I put down my fork.

"I talked to Dr. Allen and other moms online who are going through the same things and think this is for the best." She crosses her arms, elbows resting on the table. Her blonde hair is graying, flattened, and her eyes have the erratic glean of sleeplessness.

"Moms going through this thing?" I put my plate in the sink, feeling the calories unfold in my stomach, feeling them start to swell.

"With kids going through what you are I mean."

"So you'll talk to strangers on the internet about me. But not to me?"

"That is what I'm trying to do, honey. Talk to you."

"Right," I say, retreating up the stairs. Her footsteps follow me, just enough to see that I end up in my room, before receding. When I come back down later there is a new whiteboard tacked crookedly next to the kitchen window. *House Rules*, it says.

1. *Exercise is to be limited to 30 minutes per day.*
2. *Bathrooms will be off limits for 30 minutes after mealtimes.*
3. *Mealtimes will be limited to one hour. The plate's contents must be consumed in this time.*
4. *Scales are no longer permitted in the house.*
5. *Successfully following rules will result in receipt of*

*weekly allowance. Failure will result in rescinding of*
*allowance, video game time, and anything else deemed*
*appropriate.*

All this from the woman who didn't notice I lost fifty-five pounds. Who didn't realize I was throwing up after every meal I ate, when I ate. Who never talked about how everything changed this year with Jason gone and with Collin not talking to me and with everything that happened with Caila.

I text Collin, again, even though it's the fourteenth text in a row that he will not answer, following a "K" from him and thirty-seven other unanswered texts from me. A "K" is especially bad from Collin since I know it kills him to not say something like, "duly noted, young sir" or "I have taken heed, many thanks." I put down my phone, staring at the laptop, wishing he would come over so we could play *Starvation*, him lobbing creative insults, me getting distracted by the world-building and architecture, both of us eventually being eaten by zombies.

Caila, on the other hand, has been the one sending *me* numerous unanswered texts. They start off apologetic and morph into desperate. "Are you okay?" and "Please answer me," and just "Wes." Not that I don't expect this from her. I have never seen her break eye contact to twirl her hair around her finger, unlike every other girl I've dated who seems to think coy is synonymous with girly. Not that there's anything wrong with coy, it's just not Caila. In the same way vanilla ice cream is not Caila as much as rich, dark chocolate or the way darkness is not her as much as the constellations poking out, as random as they are ordered.

I still don't text back though, as much as I want to. As much as I want to hold her and breathe into her auburn hair and kiss each freckle dotting her cheeks and believe that she has changed. That she is good for me now.

# 6
# BEFORE

After I followed her back on Instagram, Caila started messaging me. Luckily, she was not a don't-text-back-right-away-because-heaven-forbid-you-show-actual-interest-in-the-other-person kind of girl. Other than that, I didn't know too much about her, except that she liked country music and was a ballerina, which seemed incompatible to me but apparently weren't. But she only liked 2000s country, not the new stuff, and definitely not anything with Blake Shelton or Miranda Lambert.

When I asked her if she had siblings, she replied: *don't you think family is a weird concept? that you're supposed to love people just because you have similar DNA, no matter what?*

Collin might have launched into a philosophical tirade about what it means to be related and what love is. Jason would have made a joke about how he didn't realize he was supposed to love me. I messaged back: *I'm sorry*—even though I didn't yet know about what happened to her brother and how she tried to hate him instead of hating herself because no one replied like that to a question like this unless there was no good answer.

I sat with my phone, typing then deleting then typing again, for some time. I finally settled on: *If you're up for it, I'd love to hear more face-to-face* and sent it before I could talk myself out of it.

She sent a smiling emoji, replying with the typical lack of capitalization: *smooth. how about a movie on Friday?*

Me: *Sure. I can do any time after 7:00.*

Caila: *there's a rom com at 7:35 at the AMC.*

I went into Jason's room to ask him what one wears to a date, especially with a strange ballerina. He was busy dusting off his trophies, which I could tell from his reluctance was Dad's idea.

"Hey," he said, standing up.

"Hey." I sat on the bed, looking at everything besides the trophies. Thinking that if I had as many as him, I would gladly dust them as often as needed.

"Sorry about dinner. Dad didn't mean anything by it." Jason sat next to me, giving my arm a soft, peace-offering punch.

"Sure he did, but whatever." I lay back on his bed, on the lumpy comforter covered in toy trucks in aggressive pastels.

"You know it isn't always easy for me either, right? The pressure?"

I shrugged. "I guess not."

Something fell on my stomach. I picked my head up, touching the Stanford sweatshirt Jason'd had for years that was now draped over me. The sleeves were pilled, the fabric worn and thin, but it smelled like home. Like burrowing next to Jason as the cold rain pelted the roof and thunder exploded angrily above and even so, feeling safe. Like laughing, teary-eyed and endlessly, about everything and nothing.

"You should have this. I can get another at the bookstore or whatever."

"Thanks," I said, grinning as I pulled it on.

Jason lay down next to me, both of us examining the ceiling. I had memorized this map of cracks and bulges, like rivers and mountains, plowing through water-stained plaster. Instead of the whispering wind, though, the only sound was of Jason's soft exhales and of the creaking roof.

"Have you ever thought about cutting weight for wrestling?" I asked, as much to the plaster rivers as to Jason.

He sat up to look at me. "It's not worth it. I mean, some people do it, but it can be really dangerous."

"Yeah, you're probably right." I wondered if he would say the same thing if he didn't have trophies to dust off.

# 7
# AFTER

Mom inches the green Volvo up to the edge of the curb, dropping me off in the one-story building labeled Simmons, Erica PhD. Below it, several awards are taped up, including Best Therapist for Eating Disorders (St. Paul Pioneer Press) and Best Women Therapists (Star Tribune).

"I'll pick you up after my meeting." She grips the wheel tightly, looking over my shoulder repeatedly.

"Okay. Which meeting, again?" I ask, tugging on the door handle.

"It's for the Johnson's new 'man-cave'." Mom rolls her eyes at the word, but I give a small smile and close the door before she can rant about the gender norms these types of words enforce and how unfair it is that there are no woman-caves and that this was further proof of the patriarchy. I had heard that speech more than enough for one lifetime.

I stand on the curb, contemplating running the opposite way or standing in the below-zero temperature for the entire hour, instead. But the Volvo is still running, still breathing in spurts behind me and I know it will not drive away until I am inside and out of view.

The cold of the metal door handle bites through my gloves, but the warm air rushes out to greet me as I step inside. It is not all glass and white tile and sterility reminiscent of a horror hospital movie like I had expected. Instead, the carpet is a textured green with a path worn down the center. The walls are a warm beige, the lights softer than the aggressive fluorescents I associate with medical institutions. Even the doors are homey. Deep wood with small inlets of glass, the one on the left engraved with Dr. Simmons' name.

I don't even think about how easy it would be to wait the entire time in the hallway or turn around and sit on the curb. My hand finds the handle and I am in and walking to the front desk and saying, "Wes McCoy" and being given papers to fill out and sitting in the chair, pen in hand, all before I realize what has happened. A part of me thinks this is because of Jason, a part of me thinks maybe it's because of me.

There is not enough time to overanalyze, though, because as soon as I finish the fourth sheet, a woman opens the door to the back and calls my name. She is relatively young with dark hair partitioned off into braids. Her dark red lips match her dark red glasses, although I'm not sure if they are a necessity or a fashion statement.

Dr. Simmons' office is small, with one black leather couch and one lone green chair. Her desk is pushed into the corner. She motions for me to sit on the couch, so I unwrap myself from my coat, my hat, my gloves, my flannel. Make a pile on the seat next to me, look up and prepare for what the three of us, Dr. Simmons, my pile of clothes, and I, will discuss.

But instead of some probing question about childhood traumas, she looks up from the notebook perched on her crossed legs and asks, "So, what do you want to talk about?"

I say, "I don't know, I didn't think I would get this far," even before I decide to say it.

She gives a small laugh. "Let me ask that another way. What brings you here?"

I slide my forefinger and thumb around my wrist, play with the hospital band that is no longer there, make sure my thumb still makes it all the way to the first crease in my finger. "My mom thought it would be a good idea."

"But you don't?"

I trace the squares of the carpet with my eyes, making patterns with the sides and the diagonals. "It's not that I don't, I just don't feel strongly about it."

"About what? Therapy? Getting better?"

"Definitely the therapy." I look up, slowly, searching her eyes for the right answers.

"And how do you feel about getting better?" Her dark eyes don't give away anything, don't tell me what I should say. They are soft, though, curved with concern.

I look outside, at the tree covering half the window with a thick trunk and dark green leaves. At the cars maneuvering like ants around the parking lot. I look back at Dr. Simmons, hoping she will rescue me from the blankness of my mind, but all she does is tilt her head a little further, waiting. "What does that even mean? Getting better?" I finally offer into the silence.

"What do you want it to mean?"

"No, really. I want to know what it looks like for me to be 'cured' or whatever." My fingers press into my wrist, twisting harder.

"Cured of what?" Her eyes scan the clipboard. Fixate. Find my eyes again.

"I don't know." I shrug. "Of not being able to eat, I guess."

Dr. Simmons readjusts her red glasses. "Not being able to? In what way?"

I look up at her, wishing she would stop asking questions she knew the answers to. "It makes me anxious."

"Why do you think so?"

I lean back into the sunken-in couch. I'm just underweight, but not like deadly underweight. Just can't eat. Don't want to. Just have to throw up when I do so the anxiety of the calories won't smother me.

When I say nothing out loud, she sets down the clipboard and leans forward. "What do you know about eating disorders?"

I shake my head. "I don't have one. I'm not a girl."

She nods, taking a moment before responding. "The gender split might be only one-to-three. At the most it's one-to-nine. It's not just a girl thing."

The skin on my wrist is turning red, itchy, but I keep my finger and thumb locked around it. Back when we were having weigh-ins I used it as a way to make sure I wasn't gaining weight, making sure my fingers could still reach a certain distance around. Now, I can't stop doing it, to make sure. To release, if only for a second, the anxiety bubbling inside me that I might have gained a pound, half a pound, an ounce.

# 8
# BEFORE

A text from Caila popped up: *random question- how good are you at math?*

Me: *Well math and I have a love-hate relationship. What kind though?*

Before I set my phone down it dinged again.

Caila: *algebra. as if numbers weren't bad enough, they had to add letters.*

Me: *I know, right? Geometry is so much better.*

There was a slight pause. I dropped my phone, playing with the fraying edge of my shirt. Ding. Caila: *so i know we're going to the movies later this week, but would you want to help me with these vicious letters/numbers?*

Me: *Of course.* I couldn't help but smile.

Caila: *not that i couldn't do it on my own...*

Me: *...But you want to see me?* I held my breath and hit send.

Caila: *maybe :P*

Me: *I'll take it.*

In an hour, I was sitting at Caribou Coffee, in the corner by the window, with my backpack and an iced coffee. I swirled the cup, listening to the ice cubes clack against the plastic.

A mother at the table across from me, her graying hair pulled into a ponytail, picked up muffin bits the little girl kept throwing onto the hardwood, all while the boy kept his water cup teetering on the edge as he talked and waved his hands dangerously close to it. As she moved the cup, the little girl smooshed a muffin into the chair next to her.

Besides the happy family, one barista stood in view, a college-aged girl with tattoos and lip piercings and a blonde-to-pink ombre of hair. On the faded couch by the sugar and straws, an elderly man slowly turned the pages of a worn-out book, his glasses almost bigger than his face.

The door jingled and I jerked my head up. Caila scanned the room, smiling as she found me. Her red hair was curled and held back by a black headband that matched black leggings and Uggs. She set her backpack in the chair across from me and bent down to give me a hug. "Hey. You want anything?"

I held up my iced coffee. "I'm good, but thanks."

Caila returned with a blended drink, piled high with whipped cream and caramel. She placed it on the table as she sat, taking my iced coffee and stealing a sip.

"Not enough caffeine and sugar in yours?" I joked.

"Mine? I got this for you. Extra whip, extra sugar." She smiled but handed me back the coffee. "Since you're the sweetest."

"Oh yeah? For what?"

Caila shrugged with a smirk. "Selflessly volunteering to help me with my math."

"Oh, yeah. Definitely selfless." I nodded with a grin.

She did the problems and I nodded that she was doing them right, even though I was too busy watching the piece of hair floating on her forehead and the slight biting of her lip and the freckles kissing her cheeks and—

"Right?" Caila looked up.

"Huh?"

"I said this should be seven, right?"

"Oh, uh yeah, right." I nodded, running my fingers through my hair.

She rolled her eyes. "It's thirty-seven. I was testing you."

My neck turned hot. "Oh yeah, I was just testing you, too." I pulled on the hem of my T-shirt, and my hair fell into my face.

Without hesitating, she reached across and brushed it away, her fingers lingering slightly before returning to her pencil.

I had to remind myself to breathe.

WHEN I GOT BACK to my room, where no trophies had appeared, there was a message from Caila, along with a picture: *did i tell you i saw luke bryan live last night? he was amazing in concert.*

In the picture, the lights of the stage glowed supernaturally around her. She looked over her shoulder, head thrown back, hair in lazy ringlets on top of her plaid shirt. Only half of her face was visible, but the expression was blank, almost worried.

*Did you have fun?* I texted back.

Caila: *i mean it was definitely cool. glad i went. not as great as coffee with you.*

Me: *But did you have fun?*

The "..." popped up. Disappeared. Popped up again.

Caila: *yeah. i did with you.* The dots disappeared. Reappeared. *at the concert- i don't know. do you ever have that feeling? where you know what you're doing is fun and you are having fun, but at the same time you kind of feel like you're looking at things from outside your body. like you're one step removed.*

Me: *Yeah, that sucks. Where no matter how close you are to people, they always feel so separate, so distant.*

Caila: *wow, exactly.*

Me: *What do you think makes you feel that way?*

Ding. Caila: *what do you think makes you feel that way?*

Me: *Touché.* I replied.

I scrolled through her Facebook, through pictures of her dancing, light and effortless, of trophies and tutus and selfies with equally beautiful friends. Concerts with dim lighting and sun dresses bathed in light. One with her holding a wiggly puppy as it licked her grinning face.

As I poised my thumb over the keyboard, trying to think of something else to say, another text popped up.

Caila: *have you ever gone on a diet? like to cut weight? my friend elizabeth was telling me she only ate fruit for a week and lost like 3 pounds.*

Me: *...I'm pretty sure that isn't healthy? Right?*

Caila: *i mean its fruit- what's unhealthy about that?*

Me: *I guess.*

Ding. Caila: *my health teacher is giving extra points to anyone writing a report on what it's like to change eating habits...but i don't think i could do it by myself.*

I picked up my phone to type. Set it back down. Picked it up again.

Caila: *would you do it with me? for science?*

I thought about how much easier it would be to win if I was wrestling smaller guys. I was only four pounds above the threshold, which meant I could do it in two weeks, less if I wanted to. If it didn't work out, I would just eat a little more the next week to make it up.

Me: *I'll do it, sure.*

I told Mom I was going out with friends for dinner because it was easier than explaining why I wouldn't eat the chicken or the salad or the bread she spent an hour making, even though it would be the first family dinner in a while that we wouldn't all be there for.

I reached into the back of my nightstand drawer, pulling out the jar stuffed with $575.37. The only money I had so far for college and life and everything else after that. Thanks, birthday money and Christmas checks and quarters found face-up. I stuffed a twenty in my pocket and walked the two miles to the grocery store, even though I couldn't feel my face by the time I got there. The refrigerators did nothing to warm me up.

The melons were too heavy to carry back and the sliced containers of them too expensive. I selected a bag of clementines, ($6.99), two bushels of bananas, ($3), two cans of pineapple, ($3.26), and a bag of honey crisp apples ($4.94). By the time I was mostly home, though, my hands frozen, fingers numb from the weight of the plastic bags digging in, I was ready to leave the fruit in a snowbank and eat an entire loaf of bread and a whole chicken.

But I had promised Caila I would try, and I had already invested eighteen dollars and nineteen cents, which was a significant enough portion of $575.37 for me to leave the bags in a bush by the back step instead, say hi to Mom reading murder mysteries at the kitchen table and to Dad unloading the dishwasher, go up to my room, wait for them to fall asleep, and retrieve the fruit. On my way back up, Jason was curled up on his bedroom floor, the door cracked open. I knocked but he didn't stir so I figured he must have fallen asleep.

The next morning, I had two bananas and an apple for breakfast. I felt healthy. Hopeful. In control. At lunch I sat next to Nate, who was telling Andre about how fraternities are an essential part of college campus culture. I got there just as he was saying, "I'm going to rush Delta Sigma Pi, just like my dad."

"You're a sophomore in high school, bro," Andre said, taking a swig of his chocolate milk.

"Never too early to plan for greatness. You know my dad—"

"Is a famous lawyer. Yadda yadda. Is changing business and the world and whatever." Andre put down his milk, rolling his eyes. "You've told us. A few times."

"Good day, McCoy." Collin punched me in the arm. "I see thou hast brought nutritious sustenance this fine afternoon."

"You know your body is your temple," I said, eliciting a few snorts.

"That's cool, man. Wish I had the self-control for that." Andre took a bite of his school pizza. The kind with the texture of cardboard and about as much flavor.

That day at practice, I felt awake. Like before I had been swimming through life and now everything was dry. My limbs seemed to move faster, everything was sharper, crisper. I found myself smiling, wishing the clock would slow down or practice would go long instead of counting down the minutes—halfway, three quarters, almost done, hang in there.

Jason even smiled at me as we were getting into the car. "Have you been practicing? You did great today."

I could barely sleep that night, my cheeks hurting from smiling, my mind clinging to all the praise, everything made so much better by something as simple as food. Something I could control in the way I had never been able to control how I wrestled or how people looked at me.

Dinner wasn't nearly as hard as I thought it was going to be either, especially with Jason on my side and Mom agreeing as long as I was eating something and as long as it was only for a week or so. I wondered if I could keep it up past then. How long my body would run on the sweet nectar of fruit. How long I could stand the constant nag of hunger, however bearable.

Caila asked me to hang out with her again: *as a thanks for doing this with me,* she'd texted.

We met at the theater on Third and Main, the one behind the old hardware store. The seats were stained with fake butter and first dates, but the tickets were cheap, and it was showing some sappy romance, and it wasn't too far from either of our houses. At least we didn't have to worry about popcorn sticking in our teeth, but I did wonder what the first date protocol on produce was—should I sneak in fruit for her? For me?

# 9
# AFTER

As the hour ends, Dr. Simmons sets down her pen. "It looks like we're going to have to finish for today. Can you do something for me for next week, though?"

I shrug.

"I'd like for you to write down things you like about your body. That could be things you like physically, like your eyes or legs for example. Or it could be things you like that your body helps you do, like play sports or cook."

I am already putting on my flannel and my coat. I cringe internally. I hate that word—body. It sounds like a squishy word or something used to describe lifeless things. Corpses, water.

"How does that sound, Wes?"

"Sure," I say, still deciding whether or not I will attempt to do it, even half-heartedly. There's nothing wrong, nothing I want to fix. I like being thin. And I still want to lose fat and gain muscle. Just a little bit more.

"And I want you to write down what you eat until we see each other again and any compensatory behaviors, like purging, you do," Dr. Simmons adds, handing me a pamphlet as I'm leaving. *What is anorexia?* it says, with a sad girl hugging herself on the cover. She's not even that thin. I shove it into my jacket pocket.

Mom is out front with the car running. "How was it?" she asks as I close the door. The Backstreet Boys are on the radio but, possibly for my sake, she refrains from doing the off-beat head-jerking she calls dancing.

I shrug since it's better than outright lying. "How is the man-cave?"

She shrugs the same way I do, but with a smile.

"Imitation is the greatest form of flattery," I reply, buckling my seatbelt.

She shrugs again and this time I'm the one who smiles.

We take a right past the horrendous townhouses. Some architect had wrongfully decided that his design should be used not only for one ugly house, but an entire army of them. All red brick with light green paint, as if a nauseated Christmas elf had thrown up on them.

Beyond them, though, are newly built Craftsmans. Each a different combination of light stone, neutrals, and a splash of color, the textures and hues blending into a masterpiece. Except I'm not looking at the stones and siding this time, but at the house two down on the left. Collin's.

The Andersons' car, a silver SUV, sits in the driveway and Collin's bedroom light, the one right above the front entrance, is on. I wonder if he's playing *Starvation* or talking with his new girlfriend or thinking about me. Or thinking about Jason. Or if he's going to forgive me for saying what I said after Jason left and I was broken and breaking and pushing him away because I wanted him to push back, to prove he was there for me no matter what.

# 10
# BEFORE

I decided to bring a banana and an apple to the movie and just eat whichever Caila didn't want. Or eat both. Or eat neither and pretend it was a joke, depending on her reaction. I left early and traffic was lighter than I expected so, after buying the tickets, I spent fifteen minutes sitting in the lobby with my phone out even though the screen was off.

Caila got there right on time, her hair straightened. She had a white knit hat that made her hair look especially red.

"Hey," she said with a smile.

"Hey. Nice to see you." I crossed my hands in front of me, taking my wrist in my other hand so we didn't have to pause awkwardly to figure out if we should hug or European-kiss on the cheek or anything.

"Did you already get the tickets?" Caila took off her hat, shaking her head so her hair danced across her shoulders. She looked at me with eyes stuck between gray and brown and green. The color as confused as her gaze was confident.

"Oh yeah, here." I dug through my pockets and handed her one of the stubs.

The theater was already dim, showing a gory and loud preview with a plot line that seemed to consist only of trying to kill as many people as possible.

I wiggled out of my coat, pulling out the apple. "Want one? It's fruit-diet friendly."

Her eyes bulged for a second before she covered it up with a small chuckle. "I already ate today, thanks."

I tucked it back into my coat pocket, hoping her words didn't imply what I thought they did. How far was she taking this diet?

I didn't watch much, if any, of the movie. About halfway through, I had worked up the courage to take her hand. She let me, but it wasn't what I was expecting. Cold instead of slick with nerves. Bones protruding instead of being softened by flesh. As if fuzz-covered instead of skin covered. I almost let go.

But there was also an electricity to her skin, one that quickened my heart rate and breathing and left my head a mess of emptiness. And there was something captivating about her perfume, deeper than just the initial fruitiness, especially when she looked at me and I felt like I imagined Jason felt when he had a trophy thrust above his head and the Stanford scholarship and a girlfriend and adoring fans.

A few minutes later, I slipped my arm around her shoulders instead, even more startled by the slenderness of her bird-like figure. The bones in her shoulders were protruding also, even though she hadn't taken off her jacket. As I rested my hand, Caila stiffened, so I set it on the seat back instead.

After the movie ended, we made our way out of the theater, the post-movie silence clogging the air between us.

"Did you like it?" I finally asked.

"Yeah, did you?" Caila pulled her hat farther down over her ears, even though it was at least ten degrees above normal room temperature in the lobby. Her freckles danced as she smiled.

"Yeah." I traced the swirls of the carpet with the toe of my shoe.

Caila chuckled. "Nice *tendu*."

"What?"

"It's a ballet move where you stretch your leg out and point your foot."

"Maybe I should be a ballerina." I arched my arms over my head and spun in a wobbly circle.

"I'd recommend ballerino, but up to you."

I rolled my eyes, but as I did, she arched her arms over her head effortlessly, and spun in a perfect circle.

"Exactly how I did it," I said sarcastically.

Her leg extended softly behind her, slipping into her hand as her back arched so from her head to her foot was a connected ring. Her eyes challenged me to replicate it as she stood upright.

"Nope. Nuh-uh. I can feel my muscles ripping just looking at that."

Caila laughed, nudging me with her elbow. "I thought you were a ballerino?"

I shrugged, leaning back into her. "So, do you want to go somewhere else? To sit or something?"

"I have to get back home." She zipped up her coat, face stoic.

My heart dropped.

"But I had fun." She caught my eyes with a smile. "I'd love to do this again."

"Yeah, me too." We walked toward the parking lot. "How's the fruit diet going?" I asked, uncertain if I should.

"Great, I've lost like five pounds so far." She crossed her arms across her chest, the first time I'd seen anything but confidence.

"In a week?" I almost stopped walking.

"Just about, yeah." Caila grinned. Freckles, dimples, pride.

"Is that healthy?"

Her eyebrows jumped in confusion. "I mean, yeah. What's unhealthy about losing weight? There's a reason basically everyone is trying to do it."

"I guess," I said as we got to her lime-green Camry. I wondered why she wanted to lose more, especially given the slight concavity of her cheeks. My eyes dropped lower, to her lips, then back up to her eyes.

"Thanks. For tonight and everything." Caila gave me a hug. Firm and certain and smelling of the strawberries dancing in her auburn hair. And so uncomfortable, so bony, so something I was not looking forward to doing again, even though she was a teenage girl who liked me and I was a teenage boy who liked her. The fruit diet had to stop.

# 11
## AFTER

When Mom and I finally get home from therapy, I spend half an hour just lying on my bed. I wrap myself up in blankets like a human burrito. I don't pick up my phone, despite the barrage of texts from Caila. Even though she's not even supposed to have her phone as an inpatient. I decide to give up on texting Collin, at least for today, especially since I can't stand the anticipation of getting a reply that is crushed more and more by every minute he doesn't respond.

I think about calling Jason, the only person who would know how to make everything right, who wouldn't have let things get this bad in the first place, but I know he won't pick up. Can't pick up. Will never again pick up. Another mistake of mine.

At least with Caila it was for her own good, for mine too. I can fix things with Collin. It isn't permanent. Unlike the collision of the semi-truck with the Volvo that overturned the car by the sludgy lake, the glass shattering like tears. And the black casket buried by flowers and sobs and too much dirt to be anything but permanent.

And instead of another trophy for State, to be polished in the bedroom next to mine, all that is left is emptiness. Especially since I knew I should have been in that car and Jason shouldn't have left that late for the State meet, and he wouldn't have, had it not been for Caila and me. The dynamic duo of destruction.

I get out my sketch pad. Carve the smoldering remains of a farmhouse into the thick, off-white paper. I drop in three chickens and two cows that are homeless and crazed, unable to handle the responsibility of being free. I curl smoke up from the blackened rubble with charcoal that coats my fingers and leaves dark fingerprints on everything I touch. Even though it doesn't make it on the page, I know the fire started from an oven, from burnt bread and pre-packaged lasagna in a paper tray.

Mom cooks lasagna for dinner, and I try not to say anything. Homemade this time, but still. None of us mention that this was Jason's favorite food. And I definitely don't mention that a slice from the side is 116 calories or that a piece from the center is 334, on average. Or that the garlic bread is 206 and the Caesar salad is 94 in the fist-sized serving on our plates.

I try not to think of these numbers, seared into my brain the way one plus one makes me think two, no matter how hard I try not to. I think of random numbers instead; 398, 12, 176, 4. But one plus one is still two and garlic bread is still 206.

"Does everything taste okay?" Mom is already halfway done with her meal but now her fork hovers over the blue rimmed plate.

"I'm not that hungry," I say. It's not the right answer. If I were polite, if I were Jason, I would say, "Everything's Great, Mom. Thank You So Much" and eat four servings of everything and not throw up any of it.

Dad's silverware clatters on the table as he breathes, the white dress shirt and striped tie rising. "I don't know why you have to make it so hard on us. Why can't you just eat? It's not that difficult."

Any other day, I would have stormed out. But I was tired of going to therapy and struggling through each meal, suffocated by stares and silence. I was tired of them thinking this was something I decided. *Okay, today you can't eat without feeling like you just missed a step on the stairs, heart skipping, breath catching, everything spinning. But tomorrow, whatever. It's not like it's a diagnosable, ongoing, mental illness.*

I push my chair out from the table, but stay seated. "You're still afraid of spiders, right Dad?"

"Yeah?" His voice is almost bored. *Get to the point.* But it's also a touch surprised, unsure.

"So why don't you just pick up a spider? Just sit in a bathtub, calmly, full of spiders. Why do you have to make it so hard on us, making us kill them for you, making us change our behavior for you? It's just a spider."

Dad loosens his tie. "Spiders are different. Lots of people are afraid of them. You need food to survive."

"Lots of people are anorexic, too, Dad. And just because we need food to survive doesn't mean it's any less anxiety-provoking for me to have to eat than it is for you to have to pick up a spider."

I shove a big bite of lasagna in my mouth, letting it dribble out the edges. "Don't even pretend you would be brave enough to do something like that—let your fear into your mouth. Swallow it. Not freak out as it pulses down your throat. Do it three times a day, maybe more."

I drop my fork so it clatters, throw my napkin on the chair, and, having made my point, having given myself the satisfaction of the semblance of control, I go to the bathroom where I promptly throw up, knowing I wasn't getting my allowance anyway.

# 12
# BEFORE

I texted Caila after I got home from our movie date: *I had fun.*
*Thanks for going with me.*

Caila: *i had fun too.*

I set my phone down, tried to close my eyes. But all I could see were her sunken-in cheeks, the yellowing of her fingernails. I texted her again: *Can I call you for a second? I have a fruit-diet question.*

"What's up?" Her voice was soft, almost a whisper. I figured she was lying down on her bed, wrapped up in pillows and blankets.

"Are you okay? Like, I know you probably have lots of people you can talk to besides some random guy you just met, but I don't know, I just wanted to make sure, I guess. That you're okay." *Wow, so poetic. Way to ramble.*

Everything went silent until she inhaled. "Yeah, I'm fine. I don't know why you'd ask."

"I'm worried you're not eating enough."

"Look, if you don't like how I look then I think we should be done seeing each other."

"I didn't mean it like that."

"Sure, whatever." The line went dead.

I went to sleep playing things over, wondering what I should have done differently, what I should do to make it up to her. I had a dream of her laughing and running through the forest. Her hair floating behind her, her body flying, weightless, over the dirt, the carefree mischief in her eyes, part gray and brown and green, and fully beautiful.

With every step she got thinner. I called out to her but the farther she ran, the quieter my voice became until she was a skeleton and the bones collapsed to the earth.

The next day I kept eating only fruit, but only because I still had enough to feed a family of four for a month. A car honked just as I took a bite of my second banana, although even the sun had not woken up yet. Even the sun was not subject to the cruelty that was the high school wrestling schedule.

I grabbed my jacket and backpack and got into Collin's silver Jeep. I took the last bite, but my stomach gurgled and I still felt empty. *You just have to get to lunch.*

"Hey, thanks for driving, Anderson." Even though it was Saturday, we still had practice and lift and conditioning and Jason was staying at Kathryn's, with our car, since her parents were at a business conference. Of course, Mom and Dad thought he was at his friend Jacob's. I figured what they didn't know couldn't hurt them.

During practice I wore a sweatshirt and sweatpants even though it was eighty degrees in the wrestling room, and by the end they had darkened with sweat. At lift I maxed on squats and bench and PR'd in sprints during conditioning. By the end I could barely move, but I couldn't stop smiling. This was what success felt like. Not the assured monotony of dusting trophies but the euphoria of sweat dripping down exhausted muscles.

I grabbed my gym bag and wiped off my face with a towel.

"Where are you guys going?" Coach yelled after the guys who had trickled into the hall. "We have weigh-ins."

*What if I haven't gone down a weight class, even after everything? What if I have?*

I just needed to go down four pounds to move down. Five to be safe. I stepped on the scale, closing my eyes. Looked down. Four and a half. Coach nodded with a smile. "Way to go, McCoy. Keep doing what you're doing."

Before I showered, I did an extra hundred sit-ups and fifty push-ups, even though everything shook. I couldn't let this feeling slip away.

When I got home, Dad was making cheeseburgers on the stovetop, the deep, meaty scent mixing with the lighter cheesiness. My mouth and aching muscles begged for one. I had an extra half pound to spare, so I decided to skip the fruit for one night. With the bun in my hands, the juice dripping onto the plate, I bit into it. The butteriness of the fat poured over my tongue, along with the warmth and thickness of the burger with the slight sweetness of the ketchup and the softness of the bun. I almost choked from swallowing everything so quickly.

Even Jason had barely taken a bite as I downed my milk, looking down at my empty plate.

"Wow, someone was hungry."

"It's not polite to comment on someone's eating habits," I said, slightly mocking. Mom used to say the same thing when we commented that it was strange baby cousin Kelly only ate blue fruit snacks or when big cousin Jeremy ate eight eggs, along with four slices of toast and bacon for breakfast.

After Jason and I did the dishes, me doing most of the work and him doing most of the talking and "emotional support" as he called it, I followed him to his room and sat on his bed.

"You're done cutting weight, right?" he asked as he handed me an XBox controller. Jason wasn't into *Starvation* but we had played *FIFA* and *Madden* together for years.

"I mean, I like food, obviously," I said, making it purposely vague.

"Good, because it's not worth it. Wrestling is only for a few years, if that. Your body is something you have for the rest of your life."

"I know," I said, stealing the ball and giving Jason a smirk.

"And you know you can stunt your growth and do all kinds of things to your digestive system. To your skin and glands and things like that. Permanent, disgusting things." Jason scored, the crowd erupting into cheers.

"Yeah, I know." I pressed the buttons harder, gritting my teeth. Hating that he spent time looking all this up.

"Good. It might not seem bad now, but it can be really

dangerous." Jason scored again on a breakaway. "Remember when I passed out after Conferences freshman year?"

I gritted my teeth, trying to take the ball back from him. "Yeah."

"Dehydration. From spitting in a cup all day."

I shrugged. "So? You're fine now, aren't you?"

Jason paused the game. "Because I stopped, Wes. And if you don't stop, I'm telling Mom and Dad."

I threw my controller on the bed. "Whatever. If you do that, I'll just tell them about you staying at Kathryn's."

Jason stood and turned off the TV. "This isn't a joke or a game or me trying to get back at you for something. Okay?"

I rolled my eyes, gripping his comforter until my knuckles went white.

# 13
# AFTER

I sleep until eleven the next morning, but it takes me an hour to get out of bed, in part because I don't want to run into Dad after the lasagna and spider thing, in part because I'm worried someone heard me throw up.

Before I get out of bed, I read over the pamphlet Dr. Simmons gave me so many times that I can quote it to myself.

*Anorexia is when an individual severely restricts their energy intake compared to what is necessary, such that their BMI falls to 18.5 or below. This may manifest itself in dieting, fasting, misuse of laxatives or diuretics, purging, or excessive exercise. Anorexia is also accompanied by an intense fear of gaining weight and disturbance in the way one's body is viewed. The main differentiation between bulimia and anorexia is BMI, especially since anorexia can have binge-purge episodes.*

The doctors wouldn't let me see the scale when they weighed me, but given the fact that the word anorexia keeps coming up, I assume I meet the BMI requirement. I wrap my fingers around my wrist, feeling the relief. That I had lost so much weight, even if it wasn't enough. That there might be a reason why all this happened, even if I'm determined not to let them "help" me. I can't, not when I know how eating will feel, how horrible it will be, three times a day, seven days a week. And I know soon they will make me eat more than my shriveled stomach can hold. They will force the food into me, jam it in until I explode or my stomach fights back with stabbing pain and enough nausea I won't be able to do anything but lay, curled up, eyes closed, praying for the waves to set me down.

I do sit-ups on the bathroom tile as the shower warms up. Sweat beads on my face. My whole body shakes and my vision blurs. I rest on my knees before starting push-ups. My arms burn, practically going numb. I step out of my boxers and hop in the shower.

I stand in the tub, eyes closed, forehead pressed to the shower wall, until the scalding water turns icy and I realize I still haven't washed my hair or anything else. I step out of the stream, quickly lathering my scalp and tipping back so my head is the only thing subjected to the freezing water.

By the time I get out, I am shaking again. I pull on a long sleeve Dri-FIT, over which I pull a flannel and then a sweatshirt. I put on two pairs of socks, my new normal. Over joggers go another pair of sweatpants. Even still I'm shivering. The thermostat says seventy-two. I turn it up to eighty even though Mom will turn it down within an hour.

Instead of going downstairs, like I know I should since it's already almost noon, I curl up on my bed and pull three blankets over me. A minute later Mom knocks and opens the door without even waiting for a reply. Which, frankly, is risky if you ask me. Not that she ever has.

"It's time for breakfast." She rests her head on the doorframe as if she doesn't have the strength to lift it. I know that feeling.

"No clients this morning?" I pull the blankets up closer to my chin, burrowing farther in.

"I was at the Jefferson's at seven-thirty and have been working on some sketches since then. Time to get up." When I say nothing, she adds, "and time for breakfast."

"I'm not hungry." I roll over so I'm face-to-face with the spider web-shaped cracks.

"Wes, it doesn't matter if you're hungry. You have to eat."

"I had breakfast already," I lie.

"Oh yeah? What did you have?"

I turn back over so I have enough time to think. I can't say anything that she would notice was missing. Nothing that I would have needed a plate for. I had made those mistakes before.

"Granola bars and an apple with peanut butter I had in my room." I keep eye contact, even when I see her expression fall and she doesn't believe me but she wants to.

"Okay, well either way, it's lunch time."

"I'm really not hungry."

"You must be hungry. I heard you throwing up last night." Her eyebrows raise. A challenge.

"I think I'm sick," I lie.

Mom leaves the room, letting the door slam behind her.

# 14
# BEFORE

After the weigh-in and the burger, I genuinely felt horrible. Besides the nausea and the bloating, I felt like I had swallowed needles. Curled up on the floor that night, trying not to moan in pain, I dialed Caila. She picked up with a snarky, "What do you want?"

"Look, I'm really sorry about earlier—ow." My stomach throbbed, taking my breath with each pulse. "Oh my gosh, ow!"

"Are you okay?" Her voice softened a little.

"I ate a burger." Breathe. "And now I think my stomach might explode."

"A whole burger? Right away? You didn't ease back into it?"

"No. I had fries and a bun, too," I said.

"Well no wonder. I mean, some people say it's just because you have to go back slowly, but I think it's a sign that we aren't supposed to eat that much. We're just accustomed to eating that much which is why it doesn't bother us, but it isn't natural."

I roll onto my back, wondering if she was being serious. "How much do you normally eat?"

"Well, usually just five saltines and black coffee for breakfast. Diet coke and an orange for lunch. Plain toast for dinner. I try to keep under two-hundred calories, unless I'm going to purge."

"Purge?" I asked, sitting up.

"Yeah, like sometimes I can't help it and I just eat a bunch, so I have to throw up. Or I have to eat because Mom makes me or whatever, so I throw up afterwards. So it doesn't get digested."

"So your parents don't know?"

"Oh, geez no. I just wear baggy clothes so they can't see and I always say I'll eat more breakfast at school. And lunch is easy because I really am at school, and dinner I usually just go to the gym or the ballet studio but tell them I'm going to a friend's house. Or if I have to stay, that's when I throw up afterwards."

"But why? I don't understand why. Aren't you hungry and miserable?"

I could feel her smile through the phone. "At first, yeah. It's horrible. I mean it's not like you think about food less—it's all I think about. But the hunger becomes almost comforting, like a sign that I'm succeeding. And at this point, eating is just awful."

"Like with the stomach pain?"

"Yeah, the pain and what not. But also just the feeling of swallowing it. Giving in to it. It's like losing control, not just over food but over yourself. And there's the anxiety that makes it hard to breathe or think anything other than how to get the calories out."

"Okay, well if you ever want to not eat dinner together, I'm always free," I said, especially since I didn't know how to respond. I wished her words didn't resonate with me. I wished I could tell her she needed to eat no matter how it felt.

"Thanks, I'll definitely take you up on that."

I pulled the phone away from my ear.

"Wait, Wes?"

"Yeah?"

"Thanks. For understanding. Most people don't."

I stared at the ceiling, trying to understand the way she thought I did, trying to come up with ways to help without hurting her more.

I fell asleep googling eating disorders. Most suggested I "get help," which was not helpful. A few inpatient hospitals came up, which I knew she would never agree to.

I looked up purging, which had around four hundred side effects. And the scariest, at least to me since I thought it was just throwing up, was irregular heartbeat and organ failure from electrolyte imbalances.

But the worst part was that most of the nutrients were already absorbed by the time they were regurgitated. In terms of calories, it basically did nothing.

I clicked on pictures. Bones so prominent I had to look close to make sure there was still skin, still eyes, still life. How could this happen? How could someone let this happen to themselves?

# 15
# AFTER

Mom comes back in the room a few minutes later with a tray overflowing with food. Toast slathered in peanut butter (170 calories), four slices of cheese wrapped in salami (140 calories, each), a glass of whole milk (103 calories), a banana (105 calories), and ten saltines (130 calories).

I look at her with pleading eyes.

"These are all bland foods, good for an upset stomach. You can eat in bed, but you have half an hour to eat all of two of these. Your choice, except one of them has to be the toast or salami."

Not the two with the most calories. Tears start running down my face. "I can't. Please don't make me do this."

Mom dries my face with her sleeve. "I know it's hard, honey, but you can do this."

She pulls out her phone and starts the stopwatch.

"What if I don't eat it?" I scan the tray again. The cold, rich milk and perfect pairing of meat and cheese. Thick, salty peanut butter on bread toasted to perfection. I think about Caila's food journal where she used to write all the foods she was craving and which she thought paired best with what and with pictures she found on the internet and recipes about how to make them.

"No allowance, no video games, and no leaving the house."

"And if I do, I get to all those things back?"

"Leaving the house, except for therapy and school, you have to earn. You already lost half your allowance last night from throwing up and not eating the lasagna, but you can have the other half and your video games, sure."

I take a bite of the toast to get it over with. The thick saltiness with the crispy softness is delicious. The kind of thing I would have, a few days ago, chewed so I could experience the euphoria of food on my taste buds, but then spit out. It was a Caila Trick, like purging and exercising and drinking a lot of water and chewing gum. I swallow the peanut butter toast, even though it sticks. "How come I'm not in inpatient if you think I'm anorexic?"

Mom straightens her deep purple blouse, kicking off the matching flats. "We don't have the money. Not with the hospital bill and the funeral and the car repair." She doesn't meet my eyes.

I take another big bite, feeling like I deserve the pain of eating, since all of those expenses are my fault.

I finish off the toast, take a swig of milk. I already feel bloated. Enlarged. Fattened up.

"Fifteen minutes," Mom says. "You're doing great."

I try to keep from rolling my eyes. Good boy, you chewed that food so well.

In my mind I wonder if the video games and half-allowance are worth it. On the one hand, being housebound means I need all the entertainment I can get. Not to mention that my measly $500 for college could use a carb-heavy diet of money for sure. On the other, complying now means more and more food that I have to eat. At least I can throw it up later. Even if it doesn't get rid of all the calories, I still feel this compulsion to do it until I feel empty and in control. Like how scratching an itch doesn't help, and you know it doesn't, but you can't help but scratch.

I down the milk because I'm already halfway through. Mom exhales.

"I need to pee." I push the covers off, almost running to the door.

Mom stands up behind me. "I'll stand outside. If you throw up, no allowance—"

"And no video games. Got it," I say.

Then, although I don't know why, "And by the way, it's not throwing up, its technically purging."

I only pee, as much as I want to feel the calories heave themselves out of me. It's just too weird with Mom right outside and I can't stand seeing her disappointment and I really need the money.

That afternoon, as I draw a tsunami consuming a town, my charcoal pencil breaks. I trek down to the basement to find a backup charcoal or a sharpener. There is barely any light except that from two light bulbs hanging from the unfinished ceiling. The floor is concrete, uneven, and dirty.

A treadmill that serves more as a laundry line than an exercise machine sits in the corner. I would have used it, before the hospitalization and everything, but I had figured it would make Mom and Dad suspicious. So instead, I'd worked out extra by going to school early or staying late at practice.

There are boxes and old furniture pieces stacked along the wall. A dilapidated bookshelf holds everything from paper to canned goods. I dig through, peeking behind green beans and three ring binders, but I don't find either charcoal or a sharpener. Some of the boxes are labeled, although I don't remember having ever opened them. *Tax Paperwork. Memorabilia. Random Crap.* I'm about to move everything to dig through *Random Crap* when I get to the box on top. *Robin's Art.* Mom did art?

The first piece I pull out is a charcoal of Dad. He has stubble and a smirk, but his eyes are softened in a smile. Beneath it is an oil painting of a mountainside. The deep greens and light yellows of the grass contrasting with the pink sunset and blue wildflowers. This was the kind of thing that should be framed and auctioned for lots of money, not tucked away in a damp, musty basement.

Underneath the canvas is an opened envelope. The paper is yellowed, but the letter inside is still legible. *Dearest Robin.* A love letter from my dad. One that gushes about her radiant blue eyes and captivating smile and the plans they had for a life together, her making millions as a painter, him as CEO of a Fortune 500 company.

I put everything back, hoist the box back onto the shelf even though it's heavy and I'm weak and it takes me a minute to catch my breath. I wonder when interior decorator became close enough to famous painter for Mom and manager of the Paper Producer Co. was close enough to famous CEO for Dad that they decided to stop aiming any higher. If I had a guess, though, I bet it was when I was born.

# 16
# BEFORE

The next morning, the burger pains had worn off, but I was enough off my game that Jason stole the first shower, even though he usually had to work his way through at least five alarms and one wake-up from Mom. Dad was just finishing off his coffee and Mom was at the kitchen island on her laptop, holding a breakfast bar.

"What's that?" I asked as I raided the cabinets.

"It's a diet bar. Supposed to cut cravings or something."

"Do you think it would help me move down a weight class?" I left out the fact that I already did, that the next one was six and a half pounds away. I let the cereal cabinet close.

"It's worth a try. Way to be dedicated, son," Dad said from behind the paper, although it took me a minute to realize he was complimenting me.

At the same time, Mom said, "Why? It's not worth it."

Dad put the paper down. "Wrestling is more than a sport, Robin. It teaches important life skills and promotes exercise. I think it's more than time Wes got more into it."

"It also promotes unhealthy weight loss, among other things," Mom added.

"So you can do diet bars but I can't?" I got out a yogurt. Checked the label—170 calories, 2 grams of fat. Not bad.

"Yes, the world is an unfair place, and do as I say, not as I do, and all that." Mom gestured in the air with her diet bar.

I poured myself a mug of coffee, skipping the normal sugar. Trying not to cringe at the bitter acidity, I downed it as Jason came downstairs. I watched as he fried three eggs, poured a bowl of Cocoa

Krispies with whole milk, and got out a banana from the fridge. I went to shower, making a mental note to look up their nutrition facts later.

As much as I wanted greasy cardboard pizza for lunch, I had a chicken salad instead, even letting myself have dressing, trying not to gag as I walked past the apples and bananas in the lunch line. I had eaten enough fruit for a lifetime.

Nate was busy doctoring his peanut butter and jelly sandwich by slipping Cheetos in between the two layers of bread. Andre was drinking one of his two chocolate milks and chowing down on his second slice of pizza. And Collin, like normal, was late. He had his Shakespearean Insult lunchbox with gems such as *"Thou art a boil, a plague sore"* and *"Away, you three-inch fool"* from which Collin loved to recite, especially to those who had no idea what they meant. He pulled out julienned carrots, which I only knew the name for since his mom had been sending them for as long as I could remember. Along with it came crackers and cheese and grapes, all in glass containers.

"Fancy meal again, Anderson. Must have taken you forever to put that together," I said, like most days, since Collin barely knew how to boil water nonetheless julienne a carrot.

He pointed to an insult on his lunchbox. I just shook my head.

Andre and Nate were in a deeply heated debate over who was the best football player which morphed into the Gatorade vs Powerade debate, when I looked up at Collin sitting across from me.

"Have you ever known anyone with an eating disorder?"

"Geez, McCoy. I knew you had problems, but really—"

I cut him off, deciding to keep the don't-make-fun-of-mental-illness-because-it's-not-a-joke lecture for later. "No, it's the ballerina I met last weekend. Caila."

"Oh, that's rough. But no, I haven't."

The fact that he didn't throw in a "thou" or a "my good sir" made me realize he didn't know how to respond.

"What do I do? She's eating like two-hundred calories a day."

"I don't know—tell her parents? I mean they have to know, don't they, but that's probably the best?"

"Yeah, you're right," I said, although I had absolutely no idea how to contact her parents or what to say.

Our wrestling meet that weekend was at another high school in the district, except this one was practically hidden in a field of corn. Luckily, there were no ballerinas this time and Jason's girlfriend, Kathryn, had to work all weekend at Victoria's Secret. Mom was there since the "man-cave" people cancelled their meeting and Dad was there because it was wrestling and he would never miss an opportunity to relive his glory days.

In the bathroom, Jason leaned over the sink, water dripping down his face.

"You okay?" I put my hand on his shoulder.

"Yeah, just feeling off today." He grabbed a paper towel and left before I could say anything else.

When I first saw my opponent, I thought there had to be a mistake. He was at least four inches shorter than me, relatively muscular, sure, but tiny. I had him pinned in seconds. And for the first time, at the end of the day, Jason wasn't the only one in first place.

I celebrated by eating half a pizza with the team afterward, even though I felt bloated and lousy by the time I got home. But it tasted so good while I was eating it, so worth the 240 calories per slice.

# 17
## AFTER

I put on my Stanford sweatshirt and lie in the middle of Jason's bedroom. The carpet is slightly crusty and trampled, but it still smells like him. I think about seeing him curled up like this, when I would wonder what he was thinking—if he was really asleep or sad or something else.

I don't try to talk to him, or his ghost or whatever, at least not out loud. The last thing I need is people thinking I'm delusional on top of everything else. If I close my eyes long enough, though, I can convince myself he's just at college, like he's supposed to be, and he's coming back soon. Or that the wind is his breath, and the sound of my heartbeat is the sound of his, too, and the warmth from the heaters is from him lying next to me. But the more I can convince myself it's true, the harder it is when I open my eyes and his bed is completely empty, and all the clothes are off the floor, and he's so actively not here.

The walls are still light blue from when Mom let us each repaint the boring beige in our rooms. Mine are green, the color of dewy grass and last-second football touchdowns and the deliciously artificial frosting on store-bought cookies. His trophies are still crammed on the same shelf, dust resting on the heads of the figurines like chronic dandruff. And on top of the papers covering the entirety of the bottom shelf, is his Stanford acceptance letter and the financial aid letter promising he wouldn't owe them anything for four years of college.

Right after the accident, Kathryn had come over to the house a few times, for family dinners that turned from stilted conversation to awkward silence, or even more awkward eruptions of tears. Even though Mom and Dad wanted to keep his belongings the same, they always let her have time alone in his room. She took two of his sweatshirts, a photo of the two of them, and the collage she had made for his last birthday. Sometimes, when I thought she had left already, I would crack open the door and see her curled up in the blankets, sobbing, with her face buried in his pillow. But eventually she stopped staying so long, stopped going up, maybe because the sheets started to lose his scent or maybe because she needed to lose the pain.

I skip breakfast by telling Dad I will eat with Mom when she gets up and telling Mom I already ate with Dad when she does. Dad goes into the office to deal with managerial things related to paper production. I don't envy him. And Mom has the last decorations for the man-cave coming in. I get out a plate, brush breadcrumbs and a drop of smeared jelly on it, flush two slices of bread down the toilet and sit at the table with the plate in front of me, reading the paper when Mom gets home. Even though I'm feeling like my limbs are attached to bowling balls and my head is feeling cotton-ball fuzzy again, it's better than the pain and pressure I feel after eating—both in my stomach and in my head. I read the Taste section three times through, stopping to close my eyes to imagine the recipes it describes. Ingrain the plates of chicken and rice and four-layer chocolate cakes in my mind for before bed, for my new sketchbook that no longer has drawings of buildings.

"You ate lunch on your own?" Mom says when she gets back at 12:30, surprised. Even more surprised when she takes out the loaf of bread and there are two less slices. "Wow, I'm so proud of you."

I smile, even though I'm crumbling inside. While she makes her lunch, the TV blaring some reality drama, I go upstairs and throw up, even though the only thing that comes out is bile and it burns. My stomach heaves to try to find something else to expel as the foul-smelling bile drips from my lips. I wipe my mouth with a Kleenex. Brush my teeth and use mouthwash. Wash my hands, stare at the ghost of a boy in the mirror, at the ugly, sunken-in cheeks and the blank expression in his eyes and the shaggy hair he doesn't care enough about to even brush. I wash my face, too, for good measure. Go and take a nap under as many blankets as I can find, even though I wake up in a cold sweat.

# 18
# BEFORE

After winning the meet, I was feeling confident in a way I hadn't before. I couldn't stop smiling. The fruit diet seemed almost worth it. I really could be a McCoy wrestler.

I asked Caila where she lived, saying I could pick her up for our next date. What I didn't say was that, really, I was going to go over to see if I could talk to her parents. I would tell them she wasn't eating and hope she wouldn't find out it was me that told them and never speak to me again. Hope they would listen to me and take it seriously.

Walking up, I was surprised Caila didn't live in a grander house. Spiral staircases and excess glass and chandeliers at the entrance. Instead, it was a brown split-level with red brick and white trim around the windows. From the size, it was likely a three-bedroom, although a fourth might have been squeezed into the basement. The driveway was made from pavers and the landscaping consisted of three barely-alive bushes lining the walkway by the front door.

The lights above the garage were off, but I rang the doorbell anyway. It was Sunday but also noon, lunch time, so I figured Caila would be gone to escape having to explain why she wasn't eating. *Please don't be home, Caila. Please don't be home.*

She opened the door wearing leggings, leg warmers, and a gauzy pink sweatshirt. The leggings were loose, floppy around her toothpick legs. Knobby, bony, toothpick legs.

"Who is it Cails?" A feminine voice yelled from behind her.

"Wes!" She yelled back, leaning on the half-open door, changing her voice to almost a whisper. "What are you doing here?"

"Um, I'm here because—I wanted to, um—surprise you."

"Oh yeah? With what?" Her hands found the pocket at the front of her sweatshirt and she shivered, despite all the clothing she wore.

"An impromptu date. I know you're not eating much but I thought we could go to a restaurant or something." *And get you to actually eat.*

"You're funny. I'll grab my coat and we can drive somewhere and sit." Most girls I knew would have tucked a strand of hair behind their ear or looked down at their feet. Caila's eye contact, however, deepened.

"Okay, but can I talk with your mom for a second first?" I took a step closer to the house.

"Wow, you really are funny. I'll meet you at the car." Caila closed the door with a smile.

I retreated to the Volvo, trying to resist the urge to bang my head on the steering wheel. *Brilliant. What a genius plan.*

It was only forty degrees, but Caila had thrown sweatpants over her leggings along with Uggs, a jacket, a hat, a scarf, and thick mittens. She climbed in the passenger seat, turning her side up to eighty and sitting on her hands as the window fogged up.

"So, you want to go to the park or something?" I asked, shifting the car into reverse.

"Sure. As long as we don't have to get out of the car."

I could feel the sweat forming on my back, even with my jacket off, as I pulled into the street. "What's your family like?"

Her eyebrows collapsed for a second, but they switched back to neutral. "I have a sister, Aria, who's older and married. My dad is a nurse and my mom is a welder and I had a brother who died from leukemia last year."

She said it all quickly, like memorized addition facts rather than something personal. Like something she had said many times to many people, in the exact same way.

"That sucks," I said as we pulled into a parking lot overlooking the lake and the two-swing swing set and, behind it, the soccer field. "What was his name?"

"Nick." She looked upward, closing her eyes and inhaling sniffles.

"We don't have to talk about it if you don't want." I turned off the headlights, unbuckled my seatbelt, turned part way to face her.

She took a deep breath. "He was so sweet. Like, all he wanted to do was laugh and give people hugs. And I remember when his hair fell out, there was a second where his face fell, but then he started grinning like, 'I'm gonna be the only one in preschool without hair. Isn't that so cool?'"

Caila wrapped her arms around herself, even though by now the heater was set to high and sweat soaked the back of my shirt. "I wasn't even that good at ballet until he got sick because I got all these free passes from my school teachers so I would skip class all the time and just go to the studio because I couldn't stand listening to an hour about protons or Washington when my little brother was dying and at least dancing I was in control of something. Of my body. Of making something that people would look at and feel something positive about. And food was the way to be better at ballet, to get that happiness and attention I didn't get while Nick was sick."

Caila finally took a deep breath. "Sorry I'm talking so much."

"Don't say sorry." I searched her eyes for the emotions she was feeling, searching her face, her cheeks.

And then she was kissing me.

# 19
# AFTER

I have therapy again. Dr. Simmons greets me with a smile and her office walls seem aggressively yellow and her bowl of chocolate on the side table seems aggressively friendly. My head throbs. I don't take off my coat this time, too cold. I hold onto the seam on the couch to make sure I don't fall over as the floor starts to spin.

"How are you doing?" Dr. Simmons asks, leaning forward to take in every precious word.

"Okay," I say.

She doesn't buy it. "Did you do the exercises I asked you to do?'

I shake my head, picking at a loose thread on my coat.

"Why not?"

I shrug. "Didn't feel like it."

"And did you purge at all this week?"

"No."

"You can tell me if you did."

I finally look up at her dark brown eyes behind bright red glasses. "I didn't."

"Can I tell you a secret?" Dr. Simmons sets down her clipboard. "I can't make you share things with me, can't make you do anything. I can't make you eat. So, you can be honest with me."

"Okay, well, honestly, I don't want to get 'better' or whatever. I like being like this."

"And why is that? What do you like about it?"

I shrug.

She sits back, crossing her legs. "Is it the control? Being skinny?"

"The control, I guess," I reply because I hate the boniness of the word skinny and the sharpness of the silence she will let us fall into if I don't reply.

"And if I could give you a way to feel in control and get to eat, but not to the point where you're overweight, would you try it?"

I shrug.

The hour takes forever to be over.

I decide to start writing down what I eat, when I purge, etc., because Dr. Simmons is right—she can't make me change what I do. And I love the control of writing it down, of knowing every amount. And the "what my body does that I like" exercise is stupid, even when we started it together—I like being able to draw. To wrestle. To imagine renovating buildings or building new ones. I like being able to wrap myself in blankets. Sleep. I write a few more things down when I get home anyway, because I've run out of natural disasters to draw and my sketchpad is out of pages and I'm bored of lying in bed and whatever, it's not like it'll make a difference.

Mom makes steak for dinner and it's no easier to eat this time. I cut the pieces into small bites, chew them excessively, wash them down with a lot of water, but by the time fifteen minutes have passed I'm not even close to halfway. Mom reminds me that I won't get my allowance or video games, but I need more sketch paper and I'm so freaking bored that I need to be able to play video games. So, even though I am panicking and my stomach feels like it can't hold any more and I can't breathe and my heart is racing, I eat the entire steak and all of the two scoops of potatoes and don't even pretend I need to pee because I know she will follow me.

"How was work, honey?" Mom looks up from her potatoes at Dad.

"Actually, pretty good. You know the SPC paper pulp contract I was telling you about? We got it finalized today. How was yours?"

"Okay. I'm almost done with the Hanson's office, which is turning out pretty well and we're about on schedule."

"How about you, Wes?" Dad cuts his steak and looks at me with eyes that are not just there to ensure food is consumed and swallowed.

I knit my eyebrows together for a second, waiting for some kind of joke.

"Okay, I guess." I put my plate in the dishwasher. "Thanks for asking."

I go upstairs and play *Starvation* even though I've never played without Collin before. I leave him three more messages: *I'm sorry. Please forgive me. I miss you.*

I see the bubbles pop up under messages, but he deletes what he's going to say and they disappear. I get eaten by zombies five minutes in. Restart the game, only make it two minutes. Chuck the controller across the room. Cover the dent in the wall with my laundry basket. I put on my jacket and hat and go outside to take a walk and realize I'm heading in the direction of Collin's house.

# 20
# BEFORE

I didn't expect Caila to do that, to lean over the stained cup holders and close her eyes and press her lips to mine, so it took me a second to realize I hadn't moved at all. Hadn't tilted my head or softened my lips or closed my eyes or whatever else I was supposed to do.

When I realized what was happening and kissed her back, the slightest bit of relief settled over me when she pulled away. Like going on the giant slide at the fair, something you try because it sounds fun, just a little bit scary, but afterward you can't help but think, *that's it?*

The sharpness of her cheeks was even sharper than I remembered.

I gave her a smile, wishing hers wasn't so genuine. What was I doing with this paper girl and her paper heart that could disintegrate at any moment?

I stared out at the lake. At the piles of snow covering it so it looked like a bare field. At the sun above and the shadows of the surrounding trees projecting onto the untouched snow. The sound of the hot air rushing out of the vents wasn't loud enough to stave off the heavy silence and I was running out of dry spots on my shirt.

"Is there anything that would convince you to eat again?" I blurted, mentally reprimanding myself for having said it.

She cocked her head to the side. "I don't know. Probably not. It's just part of who I am now."

"But have you ever thought about how things could be if it wasn't?"

"This again? Really, Wes? If you don't like that part of me, then we should be done." Caila flung open the car door and ran to the swings.

The horrible part of me said I could just wait in the car until she got cold and came back. I rolled my eyes and got out anyway, sitting on the swing beside her, carving a groove in the snow beneath me.

"I'm sorry. I'm just worried about you." I kicked snow out from under me. "And I hate that you keep saying its part of you. It's not."

"Why are you worried? I'm just going to lose another five pounds and then I'll be happy and stop."

"You promise?" I looked up from my snow trench.

"I promise." Caila stood up from the swing, arms wrapped around her shoulders. "Can we go back to the car now?"

"Sure." I walked in front of her and had my hand on the door lever when something hit me in the shoulder. I turned around and Caila had another snowball in her hand and was winding up. I ran behind the car. "Don't you dare!" I yelled, forming a snowball of my own.

I heard the crunch of her boots as she snuck closer, waiting until she was almost upon me to jump up and hit her in the stomach—just as she let hers go at my face. Bits dripped down my front, soaking the collar of my coat as my skin stung.

"Oh my gosh, I'm so sorry." Caila tried to hold back a laugh as she knelt down and brushed some of it off my cheek.

I grabbed a handful of snow and stuffed it down the back of her coat. She yelled, plucking at her clothes until it fell out the bottom. Caila pushed me backward, pinning me down and holding a large handful right above me. "Truce?"

"Truce. Yeah, truce," I pleaded, waiting until she sat up a bit to flip over, so she was pinned underneath me, instead.

I hadn't seen her eyes like that before. Shimmering with a smile, a hint of mischief. The stars across her cheeks blushed with exertion. I tried not to look at the sunken-in cheeks. At the bones pressing out. I just looked at her eyes, at the girl trapped inside. At the girl I wanted to help without knowing why or how. This girl, made of flecks of brown and green, trusted me, was not scared to look right back at me.

This time when I kissed her, when I kissed this hazel-eyed girl rather than the skeleton of her, I didn't want her to pull away.

# 21
# AFTER

It only takes me a few minutes to get to the Anderson's craftsman. It takes me almost as long to decide to pass the silver SUV and make my way up the ice-covered driveway and up the pavers and the two steps and ring the doorbell, which feels strange. Normally I just walk right in and say "hi" to his sister Greta playing with Lego in the living room and go to Collin's room and grab the controller and start playing, sometimes with Collin saying some pretentious greeting, sometimes with just a head nod.

I wait outside, though, trying to make out the distorted shapes, the Picasso life, through the flower-patterned window. Collin's mom, who insists I call her Natalie, although really I just call her Collin's mom, opens the door.

"Oh my gosh, Wes. It's so good to see you. I'm so sorry about your brother."

Then her face washes over with the expression I saw a lot after the funeral. The I-don't-know-what-to-say-now, in-fact-I-don't-even-know-if-I-should-have-brought-up-your-Dead-Brother expression. Equal parts concerned and awkward and waiting for you to say something like, "well it's been hard, but he's in a better place," so they can feel better about Death and the fact that They Will One Day Die.

I smile, say, "Thanks." Wrap my gloved hand around my other gloved wrist and turn it back and forth.

"And you're doing okay?" Her eyes find my sunken cheeks. Look down. Can't help but find them again and hold on.

"Yeah, I mean, I've been better, but I'll be okay." I give another small smile. "Thanks for asking."

Collin's mom visibly relaxes, the weight of the moral obligations and concern gone. People are so trusting, especially of hope.

Footsteps echo on the carpeted stairs behind her. Legs in black sweatpants come into view, stop. Start to retreat.

"Collin, wait." I step forward. His mom takes a step back, gesturing for me to come in. I strip off my boots, my coat, my gloves, my hat, climb two steps so I can see his face. "I'm really sorry. About everything."

He just shakes his head, glaring at the beige carpet, starting to turn away again.

"Can we just play *Starvation*? We don't have to talk or anything. I just miss hanging out with you..."

Collin is glaring less at the carpet, but still isn't looking up, isn't meeting my eyes.

"...especially since Jason died." I know it's a low blow, but I'm desperate. And it works. He looks up at me, shrugs, lets me follow him like a homeless puppy. I sit down on the unmade bed, on the side toward the window, like always.

He doesn't say anything. I try hard not to be the one who gets us killed. Try not to smile when we go ten minutes without even a close call.

Collin's phone dings. He pulls it out. "Cover us for a sec." Types quickly, replaces it. I kill two zombies, knife a third as it lunges for him. "Thanks."

"No problem. It's nice to play again."

"As if I had a choice." Collin starts laughing. "My good sir, you are horrible at not being clingy. Honestly, I thought I was going to have to change my phone number. Move to Montana or something. And you know how much I hate the cold."

I laugh but I say, "I know you're mad. I'm sorry."

"I know you're sorry."

"I'll do my best to make it up to you."

"You better, McCoy. Or I *will* move to Montana."

# 22
# BEFORE

I convinced Caila to eat more calories each day, saying it would make her body more efficient. That it would make sure she would only lose fat, keep more of the muscle. I guess it might have had some scientific relevance, but the main thing was that she was eating more. Her cheeks got a little less hollow, even though she was suspicious, panicked about gaining weight, I said it was part of the process. Gaining weight to lose more of it.

I felt like a horrible person.

I didn't know how long she would keep believing me. Hopefully long enough that I could get her some real help. But a lot of eating disorder facilities required her to sign herself in, which I know she wouldn't do, or cost a lot of money, which I knew the Brennan's didn't have.

I went over to her house most days after school, checking to make sure she was eating more. Trying to convince her to keep eating. Another bite of salad, which was healthy. Of fruit, which was healthy. But she knew too much about calorie counts and how many she had eaten that day.

I didn't want to trick her. That wasn't the goal. The goal was to get her better, healthy, so I would have more than a few months with her. More than a few years with her.

Collin and I texted more, played more *Starvation* long distance, him in his room and me in mine. A few times he came with me to Caila's house, but he had trouble talking to her, trying not to make eye contact, trying not to linger too much on the collar bones sticking out, on the thinning hair on her head and the thickening fuzz on her skin. On her rasping wheezes when we got to the top of the stairs, on her almost permanent state of shivering. On her blue lips, blue skin.

I wondered why her parents couldn't see what was happening to her, but their words were coated in a mixture of denial and helplessness, their eyes finding everything in the room besides her.

After winning the tournament, things had only gone downhill for me. I missed a few wrestling practices, especially when Caila would text me and tell me she was going to fully stop eating so I would have to go over and make sure she didn't do it. That she didn't make a habit of it. But I couldn't ensure that she was eating the rest of the day, that she wasn't just purging right after I left.

I had been so busy with Caila, in part by eating with her, that I had gone back up a weight class. So the next tournament I took fifth, which was the worst I had ever done.

Jason, unsurprisingly, qualified for state. He'd been pacing more, staying up later, and I'd seen him less and less, except at practice where he didn't seem to be any different. When I didn't qualify, I wasn't surprised either.

I skipped practice again when the news came out and went to Caila's studio. She was in a leotard, tights, and pointe shoes. I sat with my back to the mirror as she stood at the barre. I must have looked confused, probably because I was. So, she started saying the name of the moves as she did them. "*Plié*," she said, doing a squat-like thing where her feet stayed together and her knees bent out to the sides.

"*Arabesque*." Caila stood on one leg, the other extending behind her, parallel with the ground.

"*Grand jete*." Leaving the barre, she started to run to the opposite corner of the room, doing a split in midair and landing gracefully. I was in pain just watching, imagining trying to twist my body like that, open my legs that far without pulling all the muscles in my groin.

I walked over to the barre, stuck a leg out behind me, even though it bent awkwardly and barely left the floor. "Don't be too jealous."

Caila stifled a laugh. "I'm trying, Wes."

I took my foot in my hand, barely extending it as I almost fell, clutching the barre to keep from totally wiping out.

Caila covered her mouth with her hand to hide the smile, even though the laugh escaped into the air. "Impressive."

"Alright. Now your turn to wrestle." I walked toward her, feigning left and then right with a smirk.

Caila shook her head. "You wouldn't dare."

I lunged the last two steps, encircling her waist and lifting her over my shoulder. She giggled, wiggling. "Oh my gosh. Let me go!"

I spun, seeing her red curls spin in the mirrors. "Am I doing this right? The ballet thing?"

"Wes! Put me down." Her giggles betrayed her words.

I stopped spinning. "You have to tap out."

"Oh my gosh, put me down!"

"Tap out," I said again, trying not to laugh.

I set her down, letting my hands linger on her waist. On the thin fabric stretched over it. A strand of hair fell over her flushed cheek. I tucked it behind her ear, kept my fingers there.

"Nuh uh." Caila took a step back. "Not after you terrorized me."

"I did not."

"Whatever you say." She spun, one leg straight and the other bent so that foot rested on her straight knee, hands in a loop in front of her. Once she got to the far wall she kicked one foot all the way behind her, holding onto it so her leg and arm made a circle above her. Then, she ran toward me, jumping into a split in the air.

"Wow, no wonder you want to be a ballerina," I said. She was incredible. I couldn't imagine how well she would dance if she had proper nutrition, if she didn't get out of breath after a minute or two.

"Who says I want to be a ballerina?" Caila lifted her foot with one hand, extending it straight above her head. We didn't talk about the future much, since it just led to fights about how much she wanted to weigh then and how much she was eating now.

"Well, what do you want to be?"

"I want to research cancer. Children's leukemia especially." She bent her leg, let it go below her. Moved her feet a few inches, through what she told me were the five positions. They all looked basically the same to me.

"Because of Nick?" I reached for my toes, trying to feel less guilty about skipping practice by doing something exercise-related.

"Yeah. I want people to feel like they aren't completely out of control when they get diagnosed. That there's something that can be done, that will work. I mean, I want to save lives, for sure, but part of that is making it so it doesn't feel like the lottery. Trying to be the one out of ten or the one out of a hundred that survive. I want to make it ten out of ten. One hundred out of one hundred."

"That's why you eat the way you do, too, right? So you have the control you didn't have with Nick?"

"It doesn't matter why I do it." Caila did a pirouette and then what looked like a plié but while jumping.

"Sure, it does."

"Only if it's something you want to fix."

"Can we not do this?" I stood up, crossing my arms over the front of my hoodie.

"Do what?"

"Fight about whether or not you think I want to 'fix' you."

"Honestly, it's not a fight. You do want to fix me." This time after she pirouetted she kept spinning, doing three in a row until she arrived at the barre, where she leaned on it, wheezing. For a second I could see a smile bubble up.

"I don't want to fix you. What I do want, though, is for you to get better. For me to not have to worry you're going to die now or tomorrow because you won't eat."

"Oh." The color in her face drained and her eyes were unsteady. When they rolled back, exposing the whites, I realized what was happening, took two steps toward her, and caught her before her head hit the floor.

# 23
# AFTER

Collin and I kill a lot of zombies, even if we don't beat our record of making it to level thirty-seven. His mistake, trying to cross the bridge over Cibus Pass rather than going through the valley, gets us both killed, so I didn't get any heat for being "an unreliable fop, like always" or whatever.

"Want to play again?" Collin rolls his head in circles, easing out the knots. He pulls out his phone when it buzzes again.

"Whatever you want, Anderson, but I'm not covering for your texting this time."

"Oh, sorry, lad. It's Lucy." He slides it back into his pocket, clicking *New Game*.

"Lucy Martin?" I run forward, killing the first two zombies.

"Uh, yeah. We're kind of dating now." He climbs on top of a small hill, picking off zombies in the distance with a bow.

"No way. That's awesome, man. Good for you." We make it to level two, and I wish I didn't feel all the emotions I did. Glad to be playing with him again. Happy for him. Jealous he had a girlfriend and no eating disorder and no need to text me back.

"Yeah, she's utterly exceptional." He tilts his whole body, as if that will translate into the game, and barely sidesteps a zombie. I stab it and shoot the two behind him. "Sorry I haven't texted you back or anything. I know that was horrible of me to do."

I don't say anything, even with the momentary silence of moving up another level.

"It's just, my parents got divorced and you pushed me away and I don't know, I guess I didn't know what to say to you. That sounds stupid, but I was afraid of making things worse, saying the wrong thing, getting hurt myself." He doesn't add "good sir" or any Collinism as he struggles for words.

One thing I learned when I was learning about eating disorders to help Caila was that when the body gets to a certain threshold, starvation syndrome kicks in. Basically, whether it's from eating disorders or lack of access to food or whatever, starving can make you irritated, tired, and depressed. Preoccupied with food and daily rituals. Physically changed, like with brittle fingernails and the fuzz that covers the skin to keep the body from freezing. Feeling less hungry, less like you need to eat. Unable to concentrate or process things as well. Like swimming underwater where sounds are muted and distorted and slowed down and it takes twice as much energy to go anywhere.

Worst of all, the body stops sending as many "hungry" signals when it gets to a certain level of starvation, so you don't feel as hungry, even though your body is Literally Starving and You Could Die.

So you get used to eating basically nothing. You're programmed to. And you start to feel less hungry.

For those that do it, binging and purging is reinforced. You know the feeling—the euphoria of the double-chocolate chip cookie, straight out of the oven as it melts on your tongue. Except amplified because all you've been doing is thinking about this moment. Planning it, dreaming about it. And actively Not Eating the cookie. Staring at it, until you can't help it, can't stop yourself. You take a bite.

But afterward, maybe you feel a little guilty. It tastes so good, it can't be good for you, can it? And there's a reason you were holding off on eating it. But you failed. You didn't have the self-control. You weren't strong enough or good enough or whatever enough.

But then you purge. All gone. The calories couldn't have been absorbed, you tell yourself. No harm done. No negative emotions left, only the feeling of the cookie melting in your mouth.

So, the next time you are dreaming about that cookie, about any food, you remember this moment. Remember how inadequate you were, how you failed. You feel horrible. Remember how much better you felt to have the sugar coating your tongue. So you eat it. And then purge, because of the calories and the emotions and the control.

And it becomes a cycle.

Like when Collin came over after the funeral and handed me a controller and turned on the laptop and instead of thanking him for being there, or asking him to just sit with me, I yelled at him. "Don't act like everything's okay!"

I knew I shouldn't, it wasn't his fault. But it felt good to be able to be mad at someone who was still there. The way I wanted Jason to yell at me again, the way I wanted to yell at him for leaving me.

Collin had closed his eyes. "Sorry."

But I had turned away from him, holding onto the anger. "Sorry doesn't change anything."

# 24
# BEFORE

They let me ride in the ambulance with Caila. She had woken up right after I called 9-1-1, confused, trying to get away. I held her tight to me until she calmed down. Her eyes struggled to stay open, her limbs limp. She was shivering, but her leotard was still damp with sweat. I held her closer to me. I grabbed her purse as they lifted her into the ambulance, and I jumped in after her.

She was too tired to fight. Against the paramedics and the needles and the doctors. She slept most of the way there, except when she opened her eyes, confused, and I assured her she was okay. But there were some things she would fight against until her last breath.

The nurse, a shorter lady with dark hair in a low bun and round glasses, gave her a fake smile. "Okay, Ms. Brennan. We're going to insert an NG tube. It's like eating but you don't have to do anything but sit there. It'll help you get better faster."

"No." Caila picked her head slightly off the hospital pillow, shaking it as much as she could back and forth. "No nose tubes. No food. I don't want any of it."

We both knew what an NG tube was. For her, it was a way to stuff food down her throat—more than she could keep track of, more than she wanted. For me, it was the only chance for her to get to a healthy weight, give her a chance at getting out of the cycle. At getting better and keeping herself alive.

Her skin was yellowing. Even I knew that was a bad sign.

The doctor took me aside, closing the white curtain around her bed. "How old is she?"

"Fifteen. Her birthday is next month."

"Oh, hallelujah. Can you get one of her parents on the phone for me, please?"

I ducked back through the curtain, making sure Caila had fallen asleep. I pulled her phone from her purse, dialed *Mom,* and handed it to Dr. Sloane.

He stepped away for a minute before handing it back to me, nodding at the bun and glasses nurse.

"What's going on?" I asked, putting the phone back, breathing a little more now that he was standing taller, almost smiling. Hopeful.

"Since Ms. Brennan is under eighteen and her life is in imminent danger, I just need to have parental consent to continue with the NG tube insertion."

"What do you mean imminent danger?" The floor felt unsteady, the lights too hot.

"Her heartbeat is quite irregular, and I'm concerned it could progress into something worse unless we intervene immediately. Her liver is starting to fail as well, hence the yellowing of the skin. If it continues to fail, she'll need a transplant."

So, I watched as they shoved the tube down her nose. I held her hand, even though she didn't want it, tried to wiggle away from me and the nurses holding down each limb. As she hyperventilated until the nurse injected her with Valium and her eyelids started to close. I stayed with her until her parents got there, even though she could barely stay awake. Even though I knew she might not talk to me again.

I went home and took a shower, staying in until long after the hot water ran out. I put on boxers and sat on the bathroom floor until long after the tears ran out.

Someone knocked on the door and I stood.

"Wes? Are you in there?"

"Yeah," I said, my voice hitching. I blew my nose.

"Can I come in?" I imagined Jason's forehead pressed against the door. I opened it slowly.

He hugged me without saying anything. Without asking questions I couldn't answer. Questions I didn't want to think about.

"Shh. You're okay. It's okay."

He helped me get dressed. Drove me to the hospital. Stood by me when I talked to Caila's parents.

Her mother's mascara ran in inky rivers down her blush-caked cheeks. She appeared physically strong, but not overly so. Just enough that I could envision her precisely guiding a welder's torch. Her hair was choppy, like a ten-year-old had gone after it with scissors, but it fell nicely right above her collar bone.

Caila's father held her mother, still in his nursing scrubs. His face had the shadow of stubble and he was slightly pudgy, but not obese. He muttered the same thing over and over. "I'm sorry. I should have known how bad it was."

They didn't ask me if I had known. I didn't say.

Jason pulled up another chair next to Caila's hospital bed as her parents talked to the doctor. "You sure know how to pick them, Wes," he joked.

I almost laughed. I took her hand, traced my eyes over the tube that erupted from her nose, looked up at the heart monitor that had not given up yet.

"Coach isn't happy you missed another practice, even though I told him what you've been up to. And Mom and Dad are mad you've been missing so many family dinners."

"Oh man, don't tell me I missed meatloaf surprise." It was something Mom used to make when we had a lot of leftovers, taking the regular meatloaf and mixing in any chicken, turkey, or ham in the freezer.

Jason laughed. "Thankfully for all of us you didn't. But really, I know this is hard, but you can't ruin your life, too. You can be there for someone, but you can't make them better by yourself."

"I know." I rubbed my thumb over the back of her bony hand. "But I can't let her die."

# 25
## AFTER

Collin and I almost make it past level thirty-seven but a zombie gets me as I'm unsheathing my knife. He's not mad, though, just laughing.

"Really, dude? We made it that far just for you to die like that?"

"First of all, hush. I was trying to make it a fair fight," I lie. "Secondly, did you just call me dude?"

"McCoy, I would never stoop so low as to utter something like that."

"Whatever, homeskillet."

"Oh my gosh, make it stop." He clamps his hands over his ears, rolling around on his bed in fake agony.

I set down my controller, grinning. "YOLO-swag. Whatever you say homeslice. It's Gucci bae. You da real OG."

He stops, bringing his hand down in front of him. "I think my ears are bleeding."

"Good thing you're not dramatic, fam."

He sinks to the carpet on his knees, looking up at the ceiling. "Why me? Why must you torment me so?"

We both laugh, falling onto the floor.

"To be frank, though, Wes, I'm sorry about everything. J and everything else you're going through."

"The anorexia."

He says nothing.

"You can say it, you know. You can't get it from saying the word." We're splayed out on the floor. Heads almost touching, the rest of our bodies going in completely opposite directions. I can feel him relax a little, though.

"I know."

"And I'm sorry about Mittens. He sure was the fattest and best cat I've ever met."

"That he was. A right good lad."

"And sorry about your parents." I wish I had more to offer than hollow words.

"It's better this way. 'Staying together for the kids' is absurd. Doesn't help anyone to always be in a verbal warzone. Maybe this way they can at least be less unhappy." I can feel Collin shrug. I don't have any more of an idea about how things will turn out than he does.

His voice continues, softer. "I know it's none of my business and I'm sure you're flourishing or the like, but you know Jason wouldn't have wanted you to starve yourself. He didn't care how you did at wrestling."

"Yeah." I run my hands over the blue-green carpet, leaving hand tracks.

"And I realize it has progressed past cutting weight, but I just thought you might have necessitated a reminder about that."

I go back home for dinner. Eat all the fettuccini alfredo and chicken and broccoli on my plate. I do it in less than half an hour and don't try to throw up afterward. I even write down a few more things in my journal for Dr. Simmons. Because I can, because I'm in control of what I want to do and can do and will do.

Because I'm not going to die, like Jason. I'm not going to let him down again.

Most of all, I'm not going to let myself down again. I tell myself I am strong enough to eat. I need to eat. I will eat.

# 26
# BEFORE

The four of us, Jason, Caila's parents, and I, sat with Caila until visiting hours were over. When we got home, I fell onto my bed, shoes and coat still on. Jason took them off. Pulled the covers out from under me.

He crawled in next to me, pulling the blankets over both of us. There wasn't a heavy crack of thunder or the flash of lightning, like when we were little, but I still felt just as scared. Maybe even more so.

"Do you think she'll be okay?" I turned my head so we were almost face to face.

"I don't know. But it's going to have to be her choice to get better. And if she doesn't, that isn't on you. At all."

"I know, but I wish I could do more. Make her see why she needs to eat."

Jason nodded, exhaling. "But that's the hallmark of the illness, isn't it? Especially while she's this malnourished."

I shrugged. "I know. I just don't want to lose her. I would feel so responsible."

"Dub listen to me." He sat up a little. I hadn't heard that nickname in a while. It was something Grandpa had started. J and W or J and Dub. "You are not responsible for other people's choices. For the random things that happen to the people close to you."

I nodded.

"Remember that. Please. You are not responsible for whatever Caila chooses. For her getting sick. For any of it."

"Thanks, J. You should be a motivational speaker, or lawyer or something."

"Actually, Stanford has a whole major for public policy, which I think could be really beneficial for my career, especially if I go into law."

"Beneficial for your career? Really?"

"I mean, obviously I would enjoy it, too."

"Okay, your honor. Whatever you say."

"And you know they have an architecture program, so you could join me after you graduate."

"Ha, that's funny." I picked up a fuzz from the blanket, rubbing it between my fingers.

"What's funny about it?"

"Me getting into Stanford. Me paying for Stanford."

"First of all, you have great grades. As long as you do well on your ACT and essay, I don't see why you couldn't get in."

I put my hand on my forehead. "And then I can die penniless, with nothing but my degree to keep me company."

"Wow, you are dramatic."

I rolled my eyes at him.

"Anyway, there's financial aid. You could get a lot of it with how much Mom and Dad earn, and there are a lot of scholarships you can apply for."

"Yeah, I guess we'll see what happens."

I fell asleep to his soft exhales and the steady thumping of his heart, feeling like with him by me, I could do anything. Maybe even get into Stanford.

The next day I went to practice. Jason made sure I attended and made sure I apologized to Coach Worth for missing practices. He just gave me a sad, knowing nod. "It's alright McCoy. I understand. But if you want to do better, you at least need to show up."

I stood in the shower for twenty minutes afterward, everything aching, everything tired. At the hospital gift shop, I bought sunflowers and made my way up to Caila's new bed, since she was now admitted.

Mrs. Brennan stopped me outside. "Sorry, Wes, it's family only."

I held up the semi-wilted flowers. "Um, okay. Can you make sure she gets these? And tell her I came by?"

She put a hand on my shoulder. "Of course."

# 27
## AFTER

After breakfast, for which I am given strawberries on top of cheerios, skim milk, and coffee with sugar, I go back upstairs.

Tomorrow, school starts again. I'm not going, apparently. Not until I get up to a "less dangerous weight." Although I'm okay with not having to face people yet.

My new sketchpad is on the bed. Medium weight, nine-by-twelve. One side smooth for pencil, the other textured for graphite. I still have not earned the privilege to leave the house for anything other than to go to Collin's house and therapy, but I earned enough allowance money that Mom bought the sketchpad for me. Especially since Dr. Simmons says drawing is a great way to "express and explore emotions."

I go through my old sketch pads, all the way back from when all I could draw was a Christmas tree. There's one missing, though, the red, sewn binding one with all my favorite drawings. The fire-breathing dragon with scales made out of bark I found in the backyard and fire made from leftover fabric from Mom's work. A river, drawn with colored pencils, with fish distorted by the refraction of light. Jason, made from charcoal, his smug look permanently etched into the paper.

The phone rings. I keep leafing through my old drawings. Mom knocks and comes in. "It's Coach Worth, for you."

I set everything down on my lap, a conglomeration of colors and textures and emotions. "Hi, coach."

He clears his throat. "Hey, McCoy. Just checking in to see how you're doing."

"I've been better, honestly, but I'm getting healthier, for sure."

"Okay, well I just wanted you to know not to worry about wrestling. You getting healthy is more important."

"Yes, coach."

"So I'm not going to let you back to practice until you get a note from a doctor that you're back in the healthy range for weight. I don't think it's good for you to exercise too much and, frankly, I can't have you passing out on me again."

"Yes, sir. I understand." I feel even more hollow than normal.

"You're a good kid, McCoy. Sorry you have to go through this, on top of everything else. But my door is always open if you want to talk. I've unfortunately known a few kids with the same type of problems."

"Thanks, coach." I hang up. Hand the phone back to Mom. Lie down and close my eyes and try not to think about "what ifs" too much.

Mom makes tacos for lunch. Chicken and beef with lettuce, tomato, cheese, sour cream, and beans. It still feels too big for my throat to swallow, but I do it anyway. And it's a little bit easier because I don't have an excuse and I want more allowance money for more art supplies. I still think about throwing up after, about moving to Switzerland or Montana so I don't have someone making me eat. And it still feels a little like I'm eating needles, my stomach swelling, aching, but like an IV or the cut of a scalpel, it's pain that should make me feel better.

Or so they say. I'm still not sure if I buy it.

"You never told me you used to do art, Mom." I set down my half-uneaten taco.

She gives a self-conscious laugh. "Yeah, I did. Majored in it, too."

"So, why did you stop?"

"I didn't stop. I do art every day." Mom takes a sip of her coffee, lightened by cream and sugar.

"You know what I mean, though." I push around a stray diced tomato with my fork.

"If you eat your lunch, I'll show you some of my old pieces."

After we run the dishwasher, wash the pans, and wipe down the countertops she takes me up to her room, rather than down in the basement like I had expected.

From behind a rack of shoes, she pulls out a square black bag. She lays it on the bed, unzips it and pulls out three watercolors.

The first is of a black lab, head cocked to the side, with a tennis ball in its mouth. Besides the fact that I can see the slight blending of colors, the slight strokes of the brush, and the texture of the paper, it looks like a photograph.

"Wow, you did this?"

"Yep. All of these."

The next is of the Golden Gate Bridge. Photographic, too, except the edges end like clouds, not quite reaching all the way to the sides. The bridge is bright red, contrasting with the deep blue of the water below and the muted grays of the mountains in the background.

And the last one is of Jason and me, both in baby-sized tuxes. He is seated, his wispy hair standing on end above his pudgy face as he gives a grimace that was probably supposed to be a smile. I am stoic, propped up, but relatively small. I have enough dark hair that it's controlled, flat to my head.

My gaze keeps going back to the picture of the two of us. "So, you didn't stop when you had us?"

"No, I stopped when I got the interior design job. I just didn't have time for everything, and it was guaranteed income that painting would never provide."

"You should start again and sell these. You could make a lot of money."

Mom runs her hands over the edges. "Yeah... I don't know."

"Painting is an excellent way to express and explore emotions, Mom." I say, somewhat sarcastically.

She laughs. "Glad you're learning something in therapy."

"Yeah, it's either that or being bored out of my mind."

# 28
# BEFORE

State was coming up. It was all Dad and Jason talked about. I went to most practices and to the hospital most days after school even though they made me sit in the waiting room, wouldn't let me see her. In the Snapchats she sent me, her skin hovered between shades of yellow, even after her heartbeat leveled out. Most days she complained of stomach pain, but that could have been from the reintroduction of nutrients into her body.

Mrs. Brennan said Caila was gaining weight. Caila texted me that she was going crazy.

Some days I brought flowers from the gift shop, but that got to be expensive so instead I started to bring drawings. The Minneapolis/St. Paul skyline since she couldn't leave the hospital and see it. Her in her leotard, healthy and smiling, her puff of red hair floating behind her as she twirled. The lake where she attacked me with snowballs. Her house. Mine.

Lunch at school was the same as always. I had cardboard pizza some days, chicken wings others. Occasionally a salad, slathered in dressing. I thought about dieting almost every day, remembering how good it felt at the beginning, before the cravings, with the control and all the positive things everyone said. But I also knew, like Caila, I might not be able to stop if I did. Or at least I might feel like I couldn't stop.

Nate was almost done with his Cheetos peanut butter and jelly and Andre had finished his pizza and chocolate milks. Collin sat down almost halfway into lunch. "Hey, McCoy. How have you been, good sir?"

"Good, Anderson. You?"

"Superb. The only thing is I barely see my best friend anymore. Have you seen him around at all?"

"Which one is he? Dark hair, handsome? Intelligent and witty?" I took a bite of my pizza, smiling as I chewed.

"Dark hair yes, the rest, I beg to differ."

"You two coming to the state meet?" Nate shoved his empty Ziplock into his paper lunch bag.

Nate and Andre both qualified for state, along with Jason.

Collin and I very much did not.

"Of course." I nodded.

"Do you need a ride?" Andre got up to throw away his trash. His hair was starting to get long again, although nowhere near the afro he used to have.

"Nah, I'll just ride with J," I said, right as Collin said, "Sure."

He cocked his head sassily. "I see how it is, McCoy. Thou would rather spend time with thy legend of a brother than with me."

"Um, yep," I joked. "He doesn't say things like 'thy' and 'thou'."

"See if I ever play *Starvation* with you ever again, ingrate."

"I'm not too worried," I laughed.

"How's the girl?" Andre asked as he sat back down.

"Caila?" I clarified. "Better, I think. They have a tube in to make sure she's eating and all that, but they won't let me see her."

"Sucks," he said.

"Yeah, that's rough," Nate echoed.

I made it through practice, even though I kept getting distracted and Coach Worth even took me aside to ask if I was alright. I didn't even go to the hospital. I couldn't stand another afternoon of sitting in the rigid, cushionless chairs, trying to do stupid math problems and read stupid books about stupid people while Caila was just feet away, out of my reach, being forced to do the one thing she hated the most.

I went home instead, deciding to not even look at the stupid math problems, or look at the stupid books about the stupid people. I lay on my bed, throwing a tennis ball above my head, loving how strange it felt just because I was horizontal.

Jason was blasting old rock and probably pacing in his room, a leftover habit from all the meets we went to as kids, when Dad would play the same songs at full volume in the blue minivan to pump us up. Tomorrow was State. He had to be at the gym, ready to go at 9:00 am, which normally would have meant leaving at 8:00, but he insisted on 7:30.

I was going to roll out of bed at 7:20, put on sweatpants and a coat, grab a PowerBar, and go. Maybe even comb my hair if I had time. There was definitely a benefit to being mediocre. At least, that's what I told myself as I threw and caught the tennis ball while Jason prepared for greatness.

"Yo, Wes," he shouted, turning down the music slightly.

"What's up?" I yelled back, sitting up.

"Have you seen my water bottle?"

"No." I threw the tennis ball again.

He opened my door. "Cuz I saw you with it earlier. The Gatorade one with my initials on the cap."

"I don't have it."

Jason grabbed the ball from midair. "Right, whatever. It's not like the State meet is tomorrow."

"Oh really? I hadn't noticed," I said sarcastically, grabbing it back. "Next you're going to say you're a big deal or something."

"Okay, I know you're jealous or whatever, but can you just give me my water bottle back?"

I gripped the tennis ball harder, feeling it dimple in my hands. "Me? Jealous of you? Just because everyone else worships you, doesn't mean I do, too."

"Just give me the stupid water bottle."

"I know you're too cool to trust me, but I don't have it." I threw the tennis ball on the bed, brushing past him to get out into the hall.

"Right, whatever. I'd hate me, too, if I was you," he called after me.

I turned around, shoving his chest. "Eff you."

"Geez, calm down, it was just a joke." He had me in a headlock before I even realized we were wrestling. He pinned me on the floor, arm behind my back, until I tapped out.

We glared at each other through most of dinner. I glared even more when Dad said he found Jason's water bottle in the back seat of the car.

"I don't know how it got there. Did you leave it, Wes?" Jason asked.

I bit harder on my food to keep from going off on him.

"Well, did you?" J asked again.

"No, I'm too incompetent. Obviously." I spat.

Mom jumped in. "Whoa, calm down you two. Where is this coming from?"

"Real helpful, Mom. Thanks for standing up for me," I replied.

Jason rolled his eyes.

"You know, when I was a kid, my brother used to..." Dad started. Mom listened as Jason and I shoved food into our mouths.

When I went back up to my room afterwards, Jason stopped me, grabbing my arm. "I'm just stressed about tomorrow."

I shrug. "So?"

"A part of me wishes I didn't have to go. That my entire scholarship didn't ride on me being healthy and wrestling well."

I went to close the door, but he stopped it with his hand. "Wes."

"No, you don't get to be upset about this! How do you think I feel?" I almost yell. "Always being compared to you? Not even having something I can get a scholarship for?"

Jason put a hand on my shoulder. "What are you talking about? You have your art. Which is more of a sure thing than wrestling."

"Whatever. Go get your beauty sleep." I looked him up and down. "A lot of it."

He gave me a small shove.

My phone chimed. A text from Caila. *Got released from the hospital.*

# 29
## AFTER

I go to Jason's grave. I still haven't earned full privileges to leave the house, but Mom didn't stop me from going. I bring flowers. One pulled from each of Mom's potted plants in the kitchen windowsill, so it wasn't as suspicious.

Jason always thought flowers were superfluous, but I bet he would get a kick out of where they come from. His tombstone is fairly simple, not quite what a wrestling star who died young deserves, even if it was all we could afford.

The grass has mostly grown over, even though the ground is now covered with snow and ice. I am cold, shivering, but I sit down anyway, on the edge of the plot so I'm not sitting on top of him.

"Look at us," I whisper, in part to keep my volume low enough that the tears won't come, in part because it feels strange to talk to the air when I'm so used to only talking to flesh, to eyes that meet mine.

The tears come anyway.

"You, in the ground, me looking more like a skeleton than you probably do."

He, of course, says nothing.

"I'm sorry. I'm so, so sorry."

The wind blows by, chilling me further.

"You should be at Stanford. Studying public policy or whatever. Playing beer pong and kissing girls and trying to go as long as you can without doing laundry."

I set the flowers down, can almost feel him rolling his eyes, maybe even crying a little, but denying it of course. I close my eyes but all I can see is the semi hitting his car, flipping it over.

This time, though, I realize he is in the left lane. On 35E at exactly 7:45 am. It wasn't just the fact that he left late that put him exactly within the few-foot path of the semi. It was the fact that he had chosen to leave at 7:30, not 8:00 or 7:15. That he was taking 35E instead of 35W or side streets or any other road. That he was going the speed he was going so he would be right at the right spot when the semi crossed the divider and hit him.

And who's to say my making him leave a few minutes later was more to blame than the street he took? I roll my eyes at the pile of dirt.

"You're right. I'm giving myself too much credit. It's not your fault, and maybe it's not so much my fault."

I'm sure he might tell me "I told you so" or roll his eyes at me for being so slow to see it. But I also don't know exactly what he would say or do, even though people like to say things after funerals like, "he would have wanted" or "he would have said." But people are more complicated than we give them credit for, because to admit it would be to admit how little we grasp the complexities of those closest to us. Not that we don't know who they are or what makes them who they are, just that we can't know what they would think or how they would react, especially since so much of what we do is circumstantial with more factors weighed in than we know.

"But I still feel guilty, J. Because I still played a role. And I miss you."

I trace shapes in the slush in front of me, bite my lip as the shapes turn blurry.

Collin's at my house when I get home, at the kitchen table with my mom. They're drinking hot chocolate, heads leaned forward, deep in conversation. They almost don't realize I'm there, until I lean on the countertop and cross my arms.

"Hello Mother. Best friend."

"Hey, McCoy. Your mom was just telling me about how aspects of the Renaissance still influence modern day literature and art."

"Cool," I say, trying not to smile at how well they're getting along.

"Do you desire any hot chocolate?" Collin asks, as if I'm the guest. Mom starts to cringe, until I nod. He gets up, pours me a mug, and even finishes it off with whipped cream and hand-cut chocolate curls.

I take a sip. "Wow, Anderson. If the English thing doesn't work out, you should go into the culinary industry."

"I mean, it would mean financial ruin, horrible hours, and potential unfulfillment, but yeah, I would kick-ass as a cook."

I roll my eyes. "What brings you here?"

"Um, *Starvation*. Why else?"

"Wow, and here I thought it was because you enjoyed my company."

Collin shakes his head in mock sadness. "Alas, I'm just using you for your video game prowess."

# 30
# BEFORE

I went over to Caila's house, in part to escape Jason, who was freaking out about what to eat and if he should change his almost-fraying shoelaces or if they were good luck that way. I wanted to record it and send it to Andre and Nate to show them that their idol wasn't as perfect and clear-minded as they thought. Then again, they were probably freaking out, too.

Caila's parents had her propped up on the couch in the downstairs living room. Her face was washed out and she looked tired, but her cheeks were less sunken-in, which was promising. There was still a tint of yellow and her stomach was swollen, beyond the fullness of nourishment.

Mr. Brennan took me aside in the kitchen. It was comprised of old, dark wood cabinets and white appliances covered partially in dust. "Her heart has stabilized but we're having trouble getting her to eat as much as she needs to. Her liver is still struggling."

"Okay, thanks for letting me see her."

I tiptoed over to the couch, sitting down in the green chair next to it. Her eyes were closed. I sat there for a half an hour, tracing the line of her lips and the curve of her shoulder and the fan of bright red hair like a halo on the pillow.

Her eyes opened slowly. "Oh, hey."

"Hi." I took her hand, which was frigid, almost blue. "Are you cold?"

There was only one thin blanket covering her. The knit kind with all sorts of holes. And her black tank top was sleeveless. I pulled my

Hayfield High Wrestling sweatshirt off, helping guide it over her head. "Is that better or do you need another blanket?"

Her lips chattered and she shivered. "Another blanket, please."

Mr. Brennan yelled from the kitchen, "I'll get it."

I took her hand again, studying the chipped, blue-black nail polish on her nails and the fuzz on her fingers. At least I knew her body wanted to survive enough to grow its own warmth, even if it wasn't nearly enough to get her healthy again.

"Did you have dinner already?" I asked.

Caila opened her eyes. "You're on their side?"

I leaned back. "Since when are there sides?"

"Since people are trying to make me eat way more than I should be eating."

"Oh really?" I said, unable to think of anything persuasive.

"Yeah, they have me eating like thousands of calories which is insane."

"The doctors do?" I ran my thumb over the back of her hand.

"Yeah." Caila sat up a little, adjusting the pillow with her other arm.

"Almost like you need it to be healthy?" I said it slowly, so it wouldn't sound accusatory.

Caila rolled her eyes. "Like they would know!"

I sat back in the chair, hoping it would sink in for her. It didn't.

Caila fell asleep a few minutes later and I sat with her for a while. Her mom stepped in, kissing her forehead. She whispered, "Goodnight, love," before turning to me, "You heading home soon?"

I nodded, holding Caila's hand as her parents walked upstairs and turned out the lights. I sat back until my head got heavy. I closed my eyes for a second until I jumped awake. The sun fell across my face as it cut through the blinds.

I pulled out my phone. Five missed calls and twenty texts from Mom and Dad and J. It was 7:20.

An alarm clock went off upstairs. Shoot, her parents were up.

I kissed her forehead, jumped up, ran out the door, and got to our house by 7:25. I brushed my teeth, rummaged around on the floor for my Stanford sweatshirt since Caila was wearing my other one. "J, have you seen my sweatshirt?"

"Are you kidding me?" he yelled back. "I'm leaving in a minute, with or without you."

"Please, it's always so cold in the gyms." I poked my head out into the hall, but he was already running up the stairs.

"I'll look for two minutes, otherwise you have to ride with Mom and Dad." Jason punched me in the arm. "This is a lame way to become the center of attention, by the way. You could at least get a tattoo or something, really get the drama started."

"Shut up." I rolled my eyes as I dug through the laundry again.

Jason went through all my dresser drawers. "When did you have it last?"

I shot him a look. "If I knew that, I'd know where to find it, wouldn't I?"

"I don't know man, but I really have to go." Jason stood.

"Okay," I said, sitting down on my bed, surveying the explosion of clothes.

"So, you'll go with Mom and Dad?" he asked.

"Yeah. Good luck."

Jason brushed away my well-wishing. "I'm a McCoy. I don't need luck."

I rolled my eyes again, rummaging through my closet once more.

Mom, Dad, and I left half an hour later, once I found my sweatshirt on the downstairs couch and Dad put on his old Hayfield shirt and Mom finished blow drying her hair. It was raining. Thick drops that fell quickly, making a symphony on the roof and blocking the view more than a few feet in either direction. As cars went by, they sent up large plumes of water, like ski boats on a river. Dad took side streets to avoid the traffic on the freeway, but we still didn't get there until a few minutes before Jason was supposed to start.

We parked, but the only spots open were toward the back so we were soaked by the time we got inside, even after running. Coach Worth paced in the lobby and jogged up to us.

"Have you seen Jason? Is he with you?"

Dad crossed his arms. "What do you mean? He left way before we did."

I pulled out my phone and dialed his number.

"I tried that. Left ten or so messages. No response," Coach said. "He's going to have to forfeit if he's not here."

Mom's phone started ringing. She pulled it out and put it on speaker. "Jason?"

"No, ma'am. I'm sorry. There's been an accident."

# 31
# AFTER

I have to go see a doctor today. I don't remember the last time I went, especially since it costs so much without insurance, but Mom and Dr. Simmons insist I go. Mom even says someone is sponsoring me, paying for it for me. I don't know if I believe her, I can't imagine who would want to pay for me to get poked and prodded and questioned, but I'm not going to argue with free money.

Mom drives, probably as a way of ensuring I get there. We take mostly side streets like we have for the past year, but I don't mind. I like the rocking of the car as it stops and starts and seeing the tree branches shake in the wind.

I turn my seat heater on high because it's negative-ten degrees, but it feels colder.

The building looks new. There's lots of glass and the floors are a high-quality laminate. It's open concept, at least in the waiting room, and check-ins are done on iPads. There's a girl next to me, around twelve-years-old, with sunken-in cheeks and a mother who keeps touching her shoulder and adjusting her coat. Behind her is a twenty-something year-old woman with bright blue hair and a ring in her nose.

I fidget, double-checking the sign for this floor. Psychology, Eating Disorders, and Nutrition Services. Yep.

A door opens. I get ready to stand. "Kacie?" she calls out. The twelve-year-old gets up, her pigtails swinging as her mother takes her hand and leads her back. Another minute passes. Then two.

The door opens again. "Wes?" This time I get up, take as long as I can to collect my jacket from the seat next to me, and follow Mom into the overly bright hallway.

The nurse hands me a hospital gown as she shows me into a room. Before the door closes, she and Mom are already talking. I pull off everything besides my boxers and socks and throw on the gown before they can say too much about me.

"Okay, step onto the scale," the nurse says while scribbling something onto her chart. There's a post-it over the number on the scale, though. I peel off my socks first, setting them on the floor.

I stare at the scale until the nurse looks up. "You can step on."

Mom gives me a nod of encouragement. I take a deep breath, close my eyes, and step up.

The nurse uncovers the number just enough to see, but I don't even get a glimpse. "Okay, great. Hop down and we'll get your height."

I stand with my back to the wall as she lowers the stick to the top of my head. "Great. Step on out." She scribbles a few more things onto the chart. "And follow me back to the room."

I sit in the chair closest to the computer. There is an exam table, a picture of a giraffe on the wall, and a poster depicting the gastrointestinal tract. I give my date of birth and confirm that no, I don't smoke and yes, I do brush and floss and workout.

"How many times a week would you say you work out on average?" she asks, looking up at me and brushing her black hair over one shoulder.

"Like right now or before I started treatment?"

"Um, now, I guess."

"Basically, not at all. I'm not really allowed to do much."

Mom nods, so proud of me.

"Okay, I'll just put a note in and Dr. Mathison will be in in just a minute."

We wait in awkward silence. I stare at the giraffe. It stares back. A knock comes at the door and it swings open. A shorter man with gray hair opens the door, shakes our hands, and sits down, leaning forward.

"How are we doing today?"

Collin would approve of the use of the universal we. I'm still not sure what to think. "Okay, I guess." I mean, obviously I am not okay, because I'm here, but "okay" is the polite response.

"And what brings you here?" He types a few things into the computer and then looks up.

I twist my face in confusion. "Besides the anorexia?" It sounds weird to say it out loud, but the x seems a little softer and less powerful than when I hear Dr. Simmons or Mom saying it.

"Sorry, I mean can you tell me how things have progressed and how you got to the point where you're at now?"

"Um, sure." I look over at Mom, wondering if I should ask her to leave the room. I've never said any of this out loud to her.

"I can leave if you want," Mom says, reading my mind.

"No, it's okay."

So I tell him my story, starting with the diets with Caila, Caila herself, Jason's accident, restricting what I ate, purging and working out, and everything up until I passed out at practice and therapy and the house rules.

"Alright. I think it's great that you're seeing a therapist, eating more, and have family support, but I think, even though you say you can't afford inpatient care—which, ultimately, I would like you to do —more outpatient care could still provide a lot of the same services."

"And what would that entail?" Mom asks.

"They would have psychiatrists, doctors, nutritionists, nurses, and support groups, among other things. The problem, to be quite frank, is that a lot of people with eating disorders relapse, especially if we don't treat the underlying issues, and it can be hard to tell if the patients are actually doing better or are just getting better at hiding the maladaptive behaviors."

I don't say anything, even though they are both looking at me.

# 32
# BEFORE

By the time we made it to the ER, I was completely numb. They didn't say anything on the phone, but that made me even more apprehensive. Mom didn't stop talking, about everything from the worst and best cases, to the times she went to the hospital herself; for the flu, breaking her arm, giving birth to us. Dad, for once, had no degrading comment.

They led us back to the ER where a man was screaming, a baby was crying, and someone else was moaning. But we didn't stop. Dad grabbed Mom's hand, squeezing it tighter. We passed room after room, most with the curtains closed over the glass doors and full-length windows. Past nurses' stations with people in different colored scrubs answering phones, digging through files, preparing syringes, typing into computers, and talking with doctors. We entered a stairwell—the yellow paint peeling off the walls, the concrete floors worn in at the middle—and ascended a flight.

As we passed through the door, the squeak of the lever was the only sound. There was a nurses' station ahead, but only two nurses sitting calmly at the desk, leafing through files. There were no doctors clustered around, no families wandering the halls, no rooms without curtains pulled all the way shut.

"If you could wait right here, please, I'll go get Dr. Bayer." The nurse gave a small smile before scurrying off into the silence.

Mom started crying.

Dad took her in his arms. "Hey, it's okay. We don't know what happened yet. For all we know Jason could be perfectly fine."

Mom sobbed harder.

I pressed my thumb to the artery in my wrist, just to make sure I was alive, awake. I wound my fingers around it, feeling the steady pulse, the flesh. Wishing I felt nothing.

A doctor, a younger woman with curled, red hair and a stethoscope around her neck walked toward us. She gave a small, sad smile. *Don't cry. Don't cry.*

"Mr. and Mrs. McCoy?"

Mom and Dad nodded.

"I'm Dr. Bayer. Why don't you come this way, please?"

They walked forward, stiff and robotic, as if it was automatic. I supposed it had to be for them to keep moving forward.

"Why don't you tell us what's going on?" I raised my voice, staying put. *Maybe he's okay. Maybe that's why they haven't said anything. Just say he's okay so I can stop thinking of all the things that could have happened. So my stomach doesn't feel zero pounds and four hundred pounds at the exact same time.*

"Please, come this way and I'll inform you of what has happened." Dr. Bayer tilted her head with a fake smile, her curls bouncing.

"I just want to know if my brother is dead or not," I whispered.

Dr. Bayer said nothing. And in her look, in her absence of a denial, I knew.

I sunk to the floor. To the stupid, cold, tile floor under the stupid, hot lights. *This can't be happening. He was just here. No, there's been a mistake. Not Jason. He can't die. I just saw him.*

"I'm so sorry. His injuries were severe, and he has been declared brain dead."

"No." I shook my head. Shook it harder. *Wake up. Open your eyes. This has to be a dream. A nightmare.*

"I'm sorry, I know this is hard but—"

"No, you have to do something," I said louder, getting onto my knees. "Please, you have to do something. I—I can't. He's my brother."

My phone buzzed. Buzzed again. Started ringing.

"He's hooked up to a device that breathes for him to preserve his body, so he can be an organ donor."

"So he's still breathing?" I looked up, my chest lighter for a second.

"Not on his own, no. There's no chance of recovery." Dr. Bayer gave another small, fake smile. "If you want, I'll get things ready for you to see him."

We all nodded, Mom and Dad both sobbing, me feeling completely numb. I pulled out my phone, which now had twelve messages and five missed calls with voicemails. Hoping one of them was from Jason, I listened to the first. *Hi, Wes. It's Mrs. Brennan. Caila's been hospitalized and is in critical condition. The doctors want to talk to you as soon as possible, to see if you know anything. They think she might make a full recovery, but it's hard to know, so now might be a good time to say goodbye.* The phone cut out for a second, then came back on, her voice weepy. *In case it's the end.*

The other messages were all from Mrs. Brennan, too. I closed my eyes, resting my head on the wall. My life was falling apart, one person at a time.

# 33
# AFTER

D r. Mathison crosses one leg over the other, like a four. "You're still significantly underweight, Wes, which makes me concerned."

Mom opens her mouth, closes it, fighting her urge to talk, to cover up the nerves with whatever comes to mind. I try not to smile. Still significantly underweight. Just like, congrats you just won one million dollars, or have you heard crazy Aunt Susan can't make it to Thanksgiving.

"How underweight?" I ask, innocently.

Dr. Mathison barely misses a beat. "We don't like to share that information with patients, sorry."

A part of me, the weight always hanging off the back of my thoughts, whispers that I should come clean. About the missed breakfasts and lunches, the plates I brush with crumbs, throwing up on the way back from Jason's grave, behind the gnarled oak tree. Hiding food in my napkin at dinner when Mom turns away. Throwing up on the way to Collin's house. Scraping my plate into the trash and pushing it to the bottom and then sitting down, when Mom goes to the bathroom. Throwing up and missing meals and trying to lie to myself that I wasn't even doing it, blocking it out of my memory. Not telling anyone.

But the other part of me knows it won't fix anything. Just make Mom more worried and Dr. Mathison more likely to commit me to inpatient, more likely to make the family go bankrupt. More likely that I lose control over this secret that is already slipping from me. Dr. M gives us a handful of pamphlets. Inpatient places. Support groups.

Research opportunities with treatments. Websites for information and chat rooms. Tells us to come back in a few weeks.

Mom spends the whole ride home talking about the options and which seem best, which seem worst. What we can control and what we can't. How this is "Great" to have "So Many Resources" and "So Much Support." I trace the droplets on the window, merging and dividing and leaving trails as they race by. I feel like a water droplet. Pulled in too many directions until I split in half and part of me flies away before I realize what is happening. Merging with other droplets until I can't determine what is me anymore.

When we get home, I spend a few hours just lying in bed, deciding to leave everything to Mom. Hoping something will fall through and I won't have to go to any stupid therapy with stupidly optimistic people who think who I am is not who I should be.

Unfortunately, I underestimate Mom, as she already has me booked for everything by the time I finally leave my room. I should have shoved a few of the pamphlets under the seat of the car, at least the support group one.

Dad is working late. Again. Mom makes broccoli and chicken soup. Unfortunately, she doesn't go to the bathroom or turn away and she has the clock on her phone counting down the half hour. I still have broth in the bowl, three pieces of broccoli, and five minutes. I stand up.

She makes me sit back down. "Finish that or no allowance."

I need more colored pencils, but really, I just need her to think I'm getting better. So I drink half the broth. Swallow a broccoli. Stuff the other two in and the broth. Quickly put my bowl away. Walk upstairs. Spit them out in the bucket behind my laundry hamper that I will rinse out when Mom and Dad are asleep.

Mom knocks and I just barely set the bucket back and stand up before she walks in. "What are you doing?"

"I couldn't find my shirt, but I just remembered I put it in the laundry." I gesture to the bin, interlacing my fingers behind my back.

"And you had to check right after dinner? Couldn't wait until the dishes were washed?" Her eyes search behind me, around me, but find nothing.

I shrug. "I didn't want to forget."

"Okay. I want to respect your privacy." Mom shakes her head. "But if you don't get better soon, we might have to get more extreme."

I nod, as if I understand and am Totally On Board and Fighting This As Hard As I Can.

"Great. Now let's go. Support group starts in half an hour."

I glare at her back as she turns. Perfect. Just how I wanted to spend my evening. And it gets worse when I see who shows up.

# 34
# BEFORE

Dr. Bayer came back and gave a solemn nod. Mom and Dad stood and followed her down the hall. I took my time getting up. I slowly stumbled in the same direction. The longer it took for me to see Jason, the longer it would take for it to become real. Maybe if I never saw his body he would come back through the front door one morning, like nothing happened. Rub a knuckle in my hair. Say something like, "Hey, Wes. You miss me?"

I would shrug, act nonchalant until my smile deceived me and I would hug him so hard he would have to pry me off. "I knew you weren't dead," I would say. "They didn't believe me."

But I still found myself walking down the hall, turning into the room, resting my head on the doorframe. Seeing his body. The covers tucked perfectly. His dark hair brushed over his forehead. Eyes closed. But his chest was still inflating. Deflating. There was a gash cutting through his eyebrow and down his cheek and across his neck. From the doorframe, if I squinted, it almost didn't look like his face was swollen, either, nor that his tanned skin was covered in a patchwork of bruises. An impressionist painting of pain.

Mom and Dad leaned over him, obscuring my view. Mom ran her fingers through his hair. Dad put his hand on Jason's shoulder, tucking the covers in more, as if making him more comfortable would make him reconsider dying.

"I'll give you a few minutes alone," Dr. Bayer said. "And then we can discuss the organ donation."

Mom and Dad barely looked up. My phone buzzed a few more

times. I took it out of my pocket to silence it. *Please come, Wes. She's struggling to breathe. They had to intubate her.*

"Caila's in the hospital," I said, quietly.

Mom looked up, mascara running down her face. "What?"

"I think Caila might die." I pressed my palms to my eyes, taking a shaky breath. "Can I have a minute alone with J? I think I have to go see her in the hospital."

They left. I sat down next to him, took his hand. Not because it was something I normally would do, but something I felt like I should. Like in all the movies. I tried not to look at him because I was having to bite my lip harder and close my eyes, but the tears came anyway.

"I don't know what to say." I brushed his hair back into place, wiping my tears with my sleeve. "I already miss you so much."

I put my head down on his stomach. The sheets got wet below my cheeks.

"Come back." I could barely get the words out between sobs. "I don't know how to exist without you."

I gave him a hug. An awkward one, with him lying down and dead, and me unable to see much besides blurred outlines. I cried harder, knowing he would hate being hugged, being cried over.

I ran out into the hall, past Mom and Dad, wiping furiously at my eyes with my soaking sleeves. I had to stop when I got to the chipped-paint stairwell. I sat down, my chest too tight as I choked out a few breaths, my head collapsing on the paint-chipped railing, I pulled my knees into me.

A few minutes later, my torrent of sobs had ebbed to a light drizzle so I got up, checked my phone, descended a level, and made it to room 237. I stepped in the doorway. Mr. and Mrs. Brennan looked up at me. Caila lay on the bed with tubes protruding from everywhere, including her mouth. Her eyes were closed and her chest rose and fell automatically, like Jason's. I sunk to the ground.

"Hey, it's okay. We still don't know what's going to happen." Mrs.

Brennan sat down next to me, taking me into her arms. "She's sick enough to bypass the transplant lists, so there's hope."

"It's my—" I closed my eyes—"brother."

"What happened?" She stroked my hair, holding me tight.

All I could do was shake my head, sobbing.

Caila's monitor started beeping erratically, alarms going off. Nurses ran into the room, yelling, "Page Dr. Lasur!"

# 35
# AFTER

The support group meets in a conference room at the YMCA. Mom drops me off and pulls into a spot by the front door, pulling out a book. The book seems to be more of a prop, though, because she only glances at it before staring up at me as I make my way to the door. So much for an escape plan.

The carpet is worn and gray, but I can't tell if the color is intentional or a side effect of not being washed. Chairs are set up in a circle with a table in the center overflowing with organic crackers and fruit snacks and popcorn. I almost laugh. This is the kind of thing I would expect for a college club meeting, not an Anorexics Anonymous. Mom gives me a look when I call it that, but I think it's fitting. Really we are addicted to the feeling of not eating, of losing weight and losing fat. I wonder if they will give us cookies instead of sobriety tokens.

Only about half of the child-sized, blue plastic chairs in the circle around the food table are taken. I sit down on the empty side, taking in the others. There is a variety of age ranges from about twelve to about twenty-two.

Everyone else so far is female and most of them seem almost normal in weight, except one girl who stops in the doorway to catch her breath, each bone visible in her neck and face and arms. She has on a baggy dress and tights, her hair bright blue and choppy. I'm relieved when she doesn't sit next to me—she's even better at not eating than I am and a part of me resents her for it.

Two girls, slightly older than me, actually take crackers off the center table. They look like they could be sisters, one slightly shorter with a rounder face, but both with straight black hair and small noses. Neither looks underweight, so I assume they are veterans of Therapy and Support Groups and Healing. I pity them.

The leader, a woman in her thirties with leggings and a flannel, stands up. She smiles, putting her hands together. "Welcome, everyone. Nice to see you. Your body—"

"—is your temple," everyone echoes. It feels cult-y to me, like a joke.

Just as I'm thinking this, I look up. Caila walks in, her hair slightly greasy and pulled into a ponytail. She sits right next to me. "Hey."

I turn as far away from her as I can, clutching the plastic chair and grinding my teeth.

She's almost smiling, even though the happiness is tempered. "I didn't know you'd be here."

I don't say anything back. *Great. Thanks for making me do this, Mom.*

I slump farther and farther in my seat as more and more people share their stories and more and more people are crying. As soon as things end with a group hug, which I very much do not participate in, I run toward the door.

Caila grabs my hand as I'm almost outside. "Wes, wait."

"What?" I pull out of her grasp, turning my back. She is even thinner than before. I can count each collarbone, each bone in her fingers, each indentation in her skull. I feel her shiver, despite the sweatshirt, sweatpants, Uggs, winter jacket, and scarf.

She looks down at the gross gray carpet. "I'm sorry. You know that, don't you?"

I start walking again, shake my head. "Don't do this."

She catches up to me, placing a hand on my shoulder, which I shrug off. "I know I can't fix anything that happened—"

I shake my head, taking a few more steps. "You're right. You can't."

Her voice softens. "Will you at least look at me?"

I turn back, taking in her hazel eyes and her fiery ponytail and her constellation of freckles that soften as the words tumble out of her cracking lips. "I'm sorry."

I look away. At the dust-coated white laminate that does not want anything from me. At the fluorescent lights that are constant, steady. "Do you know what I would've given to have one more minute with Jason? But you tried to throw all of your damn minutes away, just like that. On the same day!"

Caila's eyes grab mine, threaten mine. "Really? Of all people I thought you'd understand it wasn't like that."

"Oh, yeah? What was it like? You couldn't stand one more minute with me? Hated what your life had become with me in it?"

For once, she looks away. "You selfish prick."

"Me, selfish? I'm not the one who tried to kill myself. I didn't take my boyfriend away from saying goodbye to his dead brother."

I don't let her reply because I'm already out the automatic sliding doors and running through the parking lot. I can feel her staring at me.

When I get in the car, Mom puts down her book. I am fuming, but when she asks how it went, I lie. I almost convince myself it's true. "Could have been worse."

# 36
# BEFORE

A nurse pushed the Brennans and me out of the room and slammed the door closed behind us. We sat in the waiting room for what felt like forever. I kept picking up magazines, reading a line or a word, putting it back down. Watching the seconds tick-tick-tick by on the hands of the clock above the door. Mrs. Brennan was sobbing. Mr. Brennan held her. I sat across from them, with nobody.

I called Mom then hung up as my first words came out with sobs. I texted instead, so it felt less real. *Caila's heart stopped.* I read the words over and over, strange words like the ingredients on processed foods. Words like benzoate and hydroxyanisole—and dying. Words my mouth couldn't find the shape of no matter how slowly I said them.

"How did this happen?" I ask. To no one and everyone.

"I don't know." Mr. Brennan strokes Mrs. Brennan's hair. The same fiery curls Caila has. "I guess she's been in a dark place for a while."

"What do you mean?" I pick up and set down Car and Driver, unread, next to all the other unread magazines.

"I mean, no one just takes that many pills on a whim," Mrs. Brennan said, wiping the tears and sitting up.

"Pills? She took pills? I thought it was the anorexia." I stood, clenching my teeth.

Mrs. Brennan put her hand on mine. "Both. The disorder started the liver failure but the pills finished it."

I pulled away, shaking my head, trying to process. "I—I need to go."

By the time I got back upstairs, Jason was already in surgery for organ donation. Even Dad was crying when I sat down between him and Mom on a waiting room loveseat that was too hard to be comfortable.

It took me a minute to realize we didn't have to wait for the surgery to be over. There wasn't anyone to wait for. But no one started to get up.

I dropped my face into my hands, trying to press the tears back into my eyes. I tilted my head back to do the same thing and focused on the peeling coffee stain in the corner of the room. I pressed my feet into the floor to keep some of the pain out of my chest so it didn't combust. When the pressure grew, I ran to the bathroom and sat with my back against the wall as my cheeks flooded and my lungs spasmed for air.

My phone buzzed four times. Rang three. I turned it off without looking and kicked the stupid white tiles on the wall, rested my forehead against them, slammed my fists into them, ran out of tears. I stayed curled up on the disgusting floor until someone knocked to use the bathroom so I got a coffee because it was warm and it felt like something I should do and I found a bench outside, tucked underneath a tree. I set the coffee on a paver, turned my phone back on. Seventeen missed calls. Ten from Mom, six from Mrs. Brennan, one from Caila's phone.

Missed texts from the Brennans: *Are you okay?*

*They got her heart restarted.*

*Her liver's failing but they found a new one. A perfect match.*

*She's in surgery now.*

Missed texts from Mom:

*Where did you go?*

*Are you okay?*

*I'm worried about you.*

*They found a patient for J's liver.*

I kicked over the cold, bitter coffee. It stained the paver, running to flow over the seams, soaking into the grass, and bubbling into the soil.

# 37
# AFTER

Collin comes over before school the next day, right after Mom positions two eggs and a piece of toast in front of me with a sadistic smile. I am sketching glass houses, tall and thin, like skinny cubes stacked on top of one another. The surroundings include sand and more sand and tan pavers. No trees for this house, no people, and just enough furniture to live in, the air demanding most of the space.

"Hey, McCoy." Collin goes to grab my toast. Realizes the gravity of such a joke, hand hovering over the offending food, face blanching.

"Hey, man. Take whatever you want." I push him slightly, enough to shake him from his trance with a thankful snort.

He sits awkwardly in the chair across from me, readjusting and sliding in and back out.

"What's up? Missed me already?" I take a bite of buttered toast. I chew it thirty times, give or take, before letting the mushy crust slither down my throat. Press my fingernails into my thighs as my throat constricts and I feel sick and oh my I need to get it out of me.

"Caila came to see me." Collin presses his fingers over his bicep, turning the dark skin lighter as he strangles it.

The surprise lets the toast sink the rest of the way down my throat. The juice I'm sipping, full of pulp and 100 calories *shoot I'm not supposed to think about calories. Think about random numbers 440. 3342, 1, 230.* It goes down the wrong pipe so I'm coughing, my lungs constricting.

When I finally stop hacking, Collin lets go of his arm. "You okay, McCoy?"

"Yeah. Wrong tube."

If I were the me from *Before*, the me from *Way-Before*, I would keep eating, stuff in an egg in two bites, let the silence prompt more answers as my brain tried to process. But of course, I'm *Right-Now* me, the one with a dead brother and an inability to even drink orange juice the right way.

"What'd she want?" I say instead, mixing the runny egg yolk around on the plate with the bent-tine fork.

Collin gives a shrug. "For you two to meet up to talk."

I lean back in my chair with a shrug as well. "Okay."

"No, like I think you should hear her out."

"Why? If she wants to starve to death, I'm not going to stop her this time."

Collin glances at my uneaten plate of food. My still-sunken cheeks. Back at the uneaten food. He stands up, slinging his backpack over one shoulder. "Well, I'm glad you're so understanding."

"I'm not the one wasting Jason's liver."

"But you are the one wasting all of Wes." Collin lets a folded note fall onto the table, shaking his head before retreating out the door.

I pick it up, running over the creases with my fingertips. Running over my name in swirly handwriting. *Wes.* The W looping at the bottom just as the S loops at the top and everything connects together, a beautiful and linked exhale.

I throw it in the trash, covering the toast and eggs, not even bothering to read the stupid, curly letters inside.

# 38
# BEFORE

The funeral was nothing short of terrible. A scratchy suit, too stiff. Standing in line, shaking hand after hand, hearing scripted condolences from an unending stream of strangers. Seeing the casket, closed because Jason no longer looked like Jason, half swollen and half discolored, sometimes in the same place. The overly hopeful speeches saturated with religious quotes Jason would have hated. The overly reverential ones saying how tragic it was he had died so early, with so much potential, so much talent, as if it would have been less tragic if he was unskilled and average. Like me.

Collin and his family were there, as was most of the wrestling team, including Coach Worth. I tried to avoid them all. They were supposed to do stupid things like punch each other in the arm, not try to keep from crying. They weren't supposed to look at me with eyes grasping desperately for the right words that didn't exist.

While everyone made their way to the grave site, I ducked behind the church. Sat down with my back against the dirty brick, knees pressed to my chest, my feet just behind the row of bushes. My hands wouldn't stop shaking, even clamped together, even stuffed under my thighs.

Wondering if I would be sitting on my bed, slaying zombies had I not given Caila my sweatshirt, had I not fallen asleep, had I not looked for the Stanford sweatshirt and just gone with Jason, had I not filled my water bottle that day at the tournament where I met Caila, had I not messaged her back, had I not gone over to her house, had she not gotten sick, had I woken up sooner in the morning.

There were just too many pieces. A giant jigsaw puzzle, perfectly constructed, perfectly out of my control, except the picture only came into focus when every single piece was fitted together, one on top of the other. If I had just controlled one, taken it away, nothing would have happened. If I just controlled something so it didn't feel like everything was inevitable and overwhelming and stupid that it was all over a sweatshirt.

Mom and Dad didn't comment about my absence when they dragged themselves up the driveway to see me crumpled on the front step, pants soaked in dirt, shirt sleeve soaked in salt.

I stood in the shower until long after I'd run out of tears and long after the water had grown icy. I laid in Jason's bed, wrapped up in all his sheets, back to the wall so I could tell myself it was him, especially with the earthiness of him all around me. When Mom called up for dinner, I turned the other way and squeezed my eyes shut.

Couldn't do something so normal as eating, couldn't let the world go on without him.

# 39
# AFTER

I go for a run when Mom goes to get groceries. I take out the trash on my way so she thinks I'm trying hard to be a Good, Obedient Son, the kind who would eat all his eggs and maybe ask for more.

Dad is getting into his car for work. He nods his approval when he sees me with the trash can and I can't remember the last time I got a nod of approval from him. Neither of us mention the person that used to take out the trash without even needing reminders.

I empty the bucket in my room into it, all the spit-up food covered by strategically placed napkins. Empty the uneaten eggs, plus four slices of toast after brushing crumbs onto a plate along with a smudge of peanut butter, a drop of jelly. Dump milk down the drain after swishing it in a glass so the suds stick to the bottom.

I open the cereal cabinet. Close it. Open it again. *Just one bite,* I beg myself, but I know it is never just one bite. *Please,* my stomach constricts. *Weak,* my brain replies.

Open, close, open, close. Down two bottles of water to try to please everyone except my taste buds, but our relationship is probably not salvageable at this point anyway.

I make sure to only run for twenty minutes so I can be done by the time Mom gets back. I doubt I could've gone longer anyway. My head throbs, I can barely breathe, and I have to sit on the edge of the bed before I have enough strength to shower. I throw my sweaty clothes at the bottom of the laundry heap and double up on socks and sweatshirts to keep out the cold that is always vibrating around me, seeping into me.

Washing my face, I scrub to get the salt off when I accidentally kick one of Jason's old action figures out from under the cupboard, and when I look up to the mirror all I see is bloated and grotesque with barely any muscle still strung across my thick bones, especially when I taste a bead of sweat cross my lips and I want a potato chip, just one, and a box of cereal, just one, and a family of four's meals for a year, just one.

When I get back to sketching, everything reminds me of food, the skyscrapers of French fries and windows of waffle squares and pretty soon I am pushing so hard the *medium-weight matte* paper is shredding. And the lime green wax pencil has broken off into a useless, colored nib and a sharp, colorless stem. I sharpen it, repair it, watch it whittle down to a portion of its former size.

I get a text from Collin. Wonder what Caila must have said to get him to be the one to text first. I leave his *Did you read it?* with no reply. Force away the urge to vilify his lack of thuses and thines with harsh, black lines that break off another nub. Reduce another pencil to a state closer to nothingness.

I press hard on my stomach when it gurgles. The cries bubbling up from a cage of nothingness. I gulp down more water to drown it—or at least quiet it a while.

# 40
# BEFORE

The first time I threw up was an accident. At least that's what I told myself. In Minnesota, and perhaps all the other human-defined areas branching off of it like the cracks in a mirror, when someone died you brought food. We had so much that the freezer was stuffed as full as we were empty, so that pans tipped out whenever the door opened, or sometimes even before.

Thus, since I had not left my room except to pee and to shower (although perhaps less than I should have) and to bring stacks of dishes down to the kitchen, I didn't notice the mold growing on the chocolate-chip banana bread until I had eaten a good chunk. I instinctively ran to the bathroom, standing over the toilet, dry-heaving. I closed my eyes, begging for the contractions to get stronger, as I felt the mold festering, growing in panicked tingles over my pulsing tongue. Clutching my stomach, I stuck a finger into my mouth, pulled it out as the breath pushed from my throat. The string of spit dripped stickily into the rippling toilet water, the stale scent of urine still clogging the air. Focused on the smell, on the way it shriveled my stomach and made the bile creep higher, I pressed the finger back more, beyond where my lungs hitched. Pushing farther, eyes closed, I coughed as everything came up at once. I choked on the burning spurts that spluttered up, splashed into the toilet in chunky, liquidy globs.

I looked up to see Mom hovering in the doorway, flushed, wiped my mouth, and rinsed with Listerine. I mumbled that the bread was moldy. I laid down on the bed with a groan and tossed and turned until the comforter came loose from the foot of the bed. I cocooned up in the middle, curled in on myself, trying not to think about how easy it had been to pull up the anxiety festering for a second in my throat. I dreamed of nothingness after finally drifting off and woke up more rested than normal.

And then, I did it again, even though the bread had no mold, after going back to wrestling and performing only slightly better than an oversized five-year-old and not nearly as well as a dead brother would. Technically, it didn't matter, being an out-of-season scrimmage. But even Coach pointed out that these things take time, but maybe going down a weight class would help, especially at the rate things were going.

School was worse, without Jason. With all the stares and whispers and nobody knowing what to say and so saying nothing at all.

I passed by Collin in the hallway. "Sorry. You know. I meant to call a bunch of times."

"It's okay," I said, instead of "I think I need you now more than ever, but I don't know what I need, because I don't know what my life is without him yet." I begged silently, *SAY SOMETHING like you normally would. Show me not everything has changed.* He gave me a solemn head-nod and was lost to the sea of people, and I felt alone as they bumped shoulders with me and stepped on my fraying Nike's.

I spent lunch sitting in the locker room, running my eyes over the chipped gold paint of the rusting locker grates, the odor of stale sweat with a hint of mold floating through the air. I threw my paper bag of neighbor-cooked pity-food in the trash then buried my head in my hands when I saw they'd already emptied his locker and took down his name sign, the outline of dust marking its absence.

I considered skipping class to sit on the football field bleachers, but when the bell rang my legs carried me to math before I realized what was happening. I absorbed nothing about tangent lines and graphing, instead I sketched snakes and crocodiles consuming zebras, looking up only when the announcements came on.

The high-pitched voice crackled above us. "Hello Hayfield.

Chess practice will be canceled after school tonight. Please plan accordingly. Volunteers are still needed for the community food drive next week. Go to the front office to register and remember this counts for those of you needing Honor Society hours. And lastly—"

For once the announcer took a breath. I put my pencil down.

"I'm sure many of you know Jason McCoy recently passed away in a tragic car accident. Faculty are always available if you need someone to talk to and psychologists will be in the back office for the next week."

As soon as the crackles clicked off, I stuffed my notebook into my backpack, throwing in my pencil. I grabbed my backpack by one strap, flinging it over my shoulder, and bolted out the door. *Don't cry. Don't cry.*

# 41
# AFTER

You'd think after losing your brother, every other day would pale in comparison. That somehow everything else would be easy. But today I sit in the car for half an hour, watching people trudge into the building, thinking about how simple it would be to turn the key and put the car in reverse.

Five minutes until classes start. I open the door and step out, zipping my coat up higher. Lock the car three times, just to be safe. Hope no one noticed I was gone. Hope they do but without noticing me.

I pull up my hood, trying to walk a little slower with a little more swagger, but it doesn't make me feel anything but more self-conscious. I go around back, to door 12C into the rear gym, but the worn brass handle doesn't budge. As I turn the corner, I get swept into the sea of coats marching toward the front door. I keep my head down, eyes on shoes. Left, right, repeat. I stop for a second when I get inside, having to remind myself what this place is, where I have to go, that I belong. I turn into the math hallway to avoid the Commons where everyone mingles and gossips and scribbles last minute homework before class. The laminate is slick, covered in half-melted snow, and the floor drops beneath me as I take a step and I'm falling and holy cow my heart is going to explode, and the room is shifting. And I catch myself. My face grows hot as my eyes lock onto Collin's and he looks away, laughing at something Andre or Nate said, but probably laughing at me, as they cluster in a circle around his locker. And when Andre takes a step back, I see Collin has his arm around someone and she's blushing, but in the cute girly way not the I-almost-wiped-out-in-front-of-all-my-friends-who-I-haven't-seen-in-forever-because-I'm-anorexic type of way. Lucy Martin. Varsity soccer. Straight, long, blonde hair. Muscular but thin, the kind of shape anyone would want.

I slide into my desk in English right as the bell rings. I wish I could hate Lucy Martin and her musculature—and Collin and Nate and Andre. But even I wouldn't say "hi" to me if I saw me, especially as I am now. Especially in front of Lucy Martin. I take my time getting out my blank, ripped-cover notebook and one stubby pencil as the announcements drone about student council and play sign-ups and dress-code reminders. My eyes stay glued on my fraying backpack even when everything is on my desk, arranged and rearranged. Footsteps thud nearby and then Andre laughs beside me as Nate snickers.

Inhale. Exhale. Andre is practically wheezing as the overhead speaker switches off.

Focus on your breathing. In for five. Hold for five. Out for five. It's supposed to make me less anxious, at least that's what Dr. Simmons says, but I think her sunny disposition still undermines her credibility, as does the fact that nothing she says actually works.

"Mr. McCoy, welcome back," Mrs. Frost says, standing up from behind her desk.

I give up on the breathing, cursing good intentions and praying to wake up or turn to Jell-o or have Joslyn's desk collapse again.

Andre lets out a snort.

"Would you like to share with the class?" Mrs. Frost takes two steps forward, skeletal arms crossed in front of her, long skirt swaying with each step.

He shakes his head with a smirk.

"Or would you like to go see Principal Hicks?"

"I'm just happy for Wes. It looks like he lost some weight."

I stand, my chair screeching as it slides back. Andre stands, face-to-face with me.

I don't inhale, or exhale, or hold my breath. He's on the floor, desk tipped over on top of him, my hands around his throat, his nails raking over my wrists, and I almost think I see something like fear, but then Nate is shoving me and I collide with a desk and fall over on it, the paneled ceiling blurring as the desk crashes to the ground. And Andre lunges for me, but some linebacker grabs him before he touches me, and a skinny kid with glasses somehow grabs Nate, and I run into the hall even though I know I might be expelled or whatever and run to the car and don't even stop to pick up my pencil stub or my ripped notebook and I can't go home yet because not even making it an hour is pathetic, even for the first day.

I sit in the car for a minute. Keys in the ignition. Engine off. I recline my chair all the way back so no one could see me if they sprinted in thanks to a broken alarm clock or the snooze function in general. So the tears pool instead of forming drops. I try to blink them away, finger encircling my wrist, even though it hurts to brush over the fingernail-shaped gashes. But at least the pain feels better there. Localized. Identifiable. Physical.

I drive past the Dairy Queen even though I want the euphoria of cold sugar. Past the Brugger's Bagels and Caribou Coffee and Cane's Chicken and Taco Bell and Vicky's Diner. I park in the abandoned lot behind the orthodontist's office and the bird food store when my vision gets blurry and my chest gets tight.

I sit there, seat heater on, temperature to eighty degrees, until the tears make my frigid body heavy and I close my eyes.

# 42
# BEFORE

After the announcement of Jason's death, I barely made it to the parking lot. I ducked under the football bleachers where Travis was smoking instead of in class, like always, his hair matted in a way where you couldn't tell whether it was intentional or accidental to have dread-like strands. The bull ring and sagging pants were supposed to make up for the lack of intimidation that would come across from a greasy, skinny boy but I guess it worked because I didn't even think about saying anything to him. I gripped a support post until it cut into my hands. I clenched my jaw, my neck, my arms, and let out a growl of sorts. It sounded stupid. I kicked the stupid post with stupid gold paint flaking off the stupid metal base on top of the stupid dirt without any stupid grass. I kicked broken bottles snuck in by stupid high schoolers, and ticket stubs, and sequins from stupid uniforms on stupid dancers.

Jason would have loved it.

How all these stupid things meant something to someone, the way his stupid trophies weren't just stupid trophies but reminders of the wrestling meet where his opponent got diarrhea midway through, or the trip to Wisconsin Dells and the first time he went down a waterslide, or the fact he was going to Get Out and Be Someone, as if he wasn't already Someone, at least to me.

And the stupidity of the timing and of the truck and the truck driver and me, for making him leave when he did, and for having to talk about him in past tense as if he no longer existed in any way in the present. As if it wasn't enough to physically lose him, but to have to lose him again every time he "was" something instead of "is" something.

I turned on my phone. Mom asked for an update. Dad reminded me to do the dishes when I got home. Four missed calls. Two from Mrs. Brennan, two from Caila And Jason's Liver. I drove to Dairy Queen and got a burger, the bun smooshed and the cheese hanging lopsidedly out one end. I ate it in the parking lot along with a mint chip blizzard but stopped halfway through. The sugar clung like scales to my cold teeth, squeezing my stomach until my tongue felt tingly, and I couldn't help but think what kind of person skipped class to eat a soggy burger and ice cream when their brother just died, and so I threw the rest out, even though together it was $7.28 and I really shouldn't have been spending anything on anything if I wanted to go to school someday, even community college.

When I got home, I parked in the driveway and unbuckled my seatbelt and rested my head on the steering wheel before getting out and walking in and preparing to make a run for the stairs. I stopped, looking back and forth between Mom and Mrs. Brennan, each with a warm mug resting between manicured hands.

Fabric swatches and paint chips and pictures of rooms too perfect for anyone to inhabit lay scattered between them. Decorating was always a great ruse to get Mom talking.

"Wes," Mrs. Brennan spoke first, her body tensing as if considering standing up. "I'm sorry about your brother."

I crossed my arms, leaning into the rigidity of the door frame with a shrug of acknowledgement.

"Caila's going home tomorrow," Mom added.

"Oh," was all that escaped in reply.

"Jason's liver saved her." Mrs. Brennan smiled, eyes glancing at the ceiling for the slightest of moments.

"I know." I dropped my stuff by the door with a thud.

Mom stood, eyebrows raised. "Is everything okay?"

I raised my eyebrows in reply.

"Right. Bad question." Mom set her mug down, palm lingering

over the rim. "I can't imagine all the things you're feeling, but it would mean a lot to the Brennans if we visited."

I bit the inside of my lip to quell the urge to swipe the coffee-stained, faded bird mugs onto the floor where they would shatter.

Shrugging, I inched toward the stairs.

"It's not your fault," Mrs. Brennan offered to my back. "And she misses you."

I stopped, hand hovering over the banister. I took the steps two at a time. I carved buildings into my sketchpad until it ripped, until the dark buildings toppled and decayed with rain. *Wasn't my fault? What did she mean by that? Of course it wasn't! I mean, I knew she was in a dark place and no one else did. But I tried to get help! But not really, not hard enough. But she was better! But you knew that meant she was just better at faking it. But she took Jason's liver! Didn't value her life! But you know as much as anyone that wasn't why she did it, lack of value. Lack of reprieve of pain, maybe, but not lack of value. But there were other things to do besides suicide! But she tried a lot of them, and you know it. Then maybe it was my fault.*

When Mom called for dinner, I rolled over and buried myself in the covers, trying to cling to sleep and the warmth of the bed in the too-cold room.

# 43
# AFTER

I jump upright to a tapping, sit up and rub my eyes to make sure there are no lingering tears. I roll down the car window to an older man with pants pulled up almost to his chest.

"I was going to say you can't park here, son." He pulls on his pants, as if they aren't high enough, as he takes in my figure, the tear stains. "But uh—take your time. No rush."

I get home, even though it's not nearly late enough for me to have finished the school day. I rush upstairs and wash my face and curl myself on my bed, covered in piles of blankets and T-shirts and semi-clean jeans. Papers overflow from the trash can, dribbling onto the floor. I wonder briefly what Caila's note said, if I should have read it. The door squeaks open then it starts to squeak closed before stopping.

"Wes?" Dad offers. "Are you under there?"

I groan.

"Rough day?"

I turn back over because that doesn't even begin to cover it. I pull the pile of clothes up closer to my chin. Dad picks a sock up from the ground and sets it on top.

"Better?" he asks.

I shake my head, trying not to smile. "Wow. So much better."

"Was someone mean?"

I shrug a little, doubtful he could see me anyway, wondering what brought this on.

"Unbelievable." He shakes his head and crosses his arms. "Just unbelievable."

"It's fine," I say, because there really is no use getting worked up about things like this.

"No, it's not fine." He ducks into the hall.

I'm confused, especially as I hear him mutter to himself along with a soft thudding.

Dad pulls Jason's chair in, setting it in front of the bed.

"You moved it?" I start to sit up, my voice getting louder.

"What?" He falls into it, leaning back.

"His chair. You moved his chair?" Socks and shirts tumble to the ground.

"Um, yes, I moved the chair. It's a chair. And it has not been used in forever."

Jeans drop to the carpet, falling on the shirts. "But it's his. *Was* his."

"Why does it matter?" Dad crosses his arms.

"Because it was his." I knock a pair of sweatpants off as I swing my legs around.

"But he's not here. Why shouldn't we move it?"

I shrug. "I don't know."

"So it feels less real?"

"I guess."

"And has it been working? Does it not feel real?"

"Obviously not—"

"Okay then. There's no reason." He stands up, crossing his arms again as he turns around in the doorway. "Unless it's not just that."

"I don't know."

"Sure you do." His hand finds the door handle.

I shrug. He stays there, eyes unwavering.

"I mean, what if we lose him?" I ask. "Or forget things?"

"Those are two very different things." Dad closes the door and the knob clicks.

The chair stays for three days until I take it out to the road, next to the trash and the recycling, with a sign, "free to a good home." It's gone within an hour and instead of feeling empty like a piece of him is missing, I feel just a little bit better. He always hated that chair.

# 44
# BEFORE

**M**om came into my room the next morning, sitting down on the bed next to me, her feet inches from the funeral suit that never made it back onto the hanger.

"I don't feel well."

She didn't even touch my forehead, ask what didn't feel well. Instead, Mom stood up, put the suit on a hanger, and stuffed it into the back of the closet. She came back with a piece of peanut butter toast, cut on the diagonal, and orange juice.

She set it next to my bed. "You can stay home, but we're going to visit Caila this afternoon."

The door shut softly. I glared at the toast. I ate half of it, even though it scratched my throat. I turned back over, lying with my eyes closed as the morning ticked away.

When I woke up again, I drained the orange juice and leaned off the bed enough to grab my sketchpad. A leg, with a pink shoe and pink tights, curved in the air. A tutu and another leg on tiptoe, holding the whole body upright. Arms arched gracefully overhead, face blissed. Curly, red hair pulled back into a bun, a few ringlets framing the ballerina's face.

On the next page, the same shape, same hair in the same bun, but the pink tutu was replaced with thick black feathers that extended over the entire body. Instead of weightless, she now seemed to struggle to retain the position with the weight of the black strips and the curvature of her own body.

I crumpled it up and threw it away. I tried again, this time with a blue first, then black to give it depth and the sheen of a crow's coat.

Caila still looked strained, her pencil body too heavy to hold itself up on paper, even after I made the feathers white, ethereal and angelic, even after I made the feathers on her arms into wings.

I threw them all away and tucked the sketchpad under the bed. I tossed and turned until Mom opened the door and told me I had twenty minutes. I turned until she came back in at fifteen and waited in the door.

"Why don't you and Dad just go?"

"This isn't about Dad and me."

I pulled the covers up higher. "Please don't make me go."

"I started the shower for you." She sat next to me on the bed.

"Please, Mom. I can't do this right now."

"I know, honey." She stroked my hair. "You shouldn't have to."

I showered, because I smelled and because I hated the way I could almost feel the germs on me. I combed my hair, brushed my teeth, pulled on a T-shirt and jeans. Then laid back on my bed, the wrong way so my legs were hanging off the side.

"Wes, time to go," Mom yelled from the bottom of the stairs.

I stood up, not because I wanted to, but because, like Mom had implied, I should. Had to, even. Because of compassion and empathy and all kinds of things I really did not want to have. Because of guilt.

I plodded out into the car and rested my head on the cold window, even though it vibrated beneath my cheek and rattled my skull.

We parked on the street then slowly made our way up to the door where Mr. Brennan was already standing, opening the door with a nod. Mrs. Brennan hugged us, leading us into the living room. There were blankets piled high in the green, upholstered chair. There was hardwood underneath and a turquoise rug and a coffee table with a glass top. Everything was perfectly placed. The rug just touching the couch and chair legs, the books on the coffee table exactly in the center, the glass fingerprint-free. Each of the blankets a perfect square, each pillow fluffed to maximum fullness.

Caila was curled up on the couch, eyes pressed tightly together.

They opened as we stepped nearer, dull and shaky, and I thought for sure they did an eye transplant instead because there was no way those were hers.

Her hair was flattened, the curls smooshed. Her skin, too, was almost clear, colorless. She was like a transparent baby bird, newly hatched, unable to take in all the stimuli. The room felt broken where she was, the perfect lines and angles cut by curves and strands and bumps. The harsh lines of her too-thin arms curled toward a too-thin face.

"Hey," she croaked, shifting to sit up.

Mrs. Brennan tensed, holding her breath.

"Thanks. For coming," Caila managed.

"Of course," Mom said. "Glad you're feeling better."

"I'm really." A breath. "Grateful for the liver." Another breath. "You know."

Both Mom and Dad nodded. I twisted my fingers back and forth around my wrist.

Mr. Brennan uncrossed his arms. "It's great having her home."

"I bet," Mom replied.

The unspoken choked me. My wrist was raw and it wasn't keeping my chest from feeling any tighter. I turned and retreated into the entrance way.

# 45
## AFTER

Dad pushes the vacuum down the hall, turning it off as I emerge.

"I can do your bedroom if you want. And I'm doing a load of laundry so you can throw your stuff in."

I tilt my head, confused by the sudden cleaning spree. On my way past, I can see the bathroom no longer has bottles strewn randomly across the counter, nor hair on the tile. I try not to be too weirded out.

Mom is sipping tea at the kitchen table as I come down the stairs. It's the kind of tea that promises to Detoxify and Heal and overall Improve Your Life. I think it tastes like dirt. What people will do for the illusion of control in their lives. Drink dirt tea. Eat nothing.

"How was school?" Mom asks, cupping her hands around the warm mug.

I pull out a chair and flop into it. I exhale as an answer.

"Work was great, thanks for asking." She takes another sip. I almost grimace for her as the liquid hits her taste buds. "And we have to leave for Dr. Mathison's in about twenty minutes."

"Ugh, do we have to?" I groan and sink my face into the table.

Mom sets her mug down. "We really should have signed you up for theater."

I shake my head to keep from smiling.

Just thinking about walking into the office, my stomach cramps. One might argue feeling sick is a good reason to see a doctor. Not me.

I can't help thinking of what they might do to me. Stupid nose tubes shoved in me in order to stuff me full as I choke on the calories, bloating and swelling. Doctors trying to reduce the swelling by making me spill my problems, so they can tape my bloated body back together enough to push me out into the world until I deflate and am wheeled back in.

I draw this image in my sketch pad, balloon people tethered by nose tubes to the ground, deflating, being dragged back, being re-inflated. In the car I try to sink into the seat, adjust the vents to drown out the silence, stare out the window, pretend I don't feel her staring at me. Pluck at the stray thread on the fraying seat covers.

I wear heavy clothes, a sweatshirt and sweatpants, but in the end it doesn't matter because they make me put on the flimsy hospital gown first, which is not going to help me in any way. I try not to notice the way Mom tenses when she sees the bony legs and arms poking out from the paper dress, as if it's the first time she's seeing them.

Dr. M isn't great at hiding his expression when he looks at the chart either, or when he takes an extra few breaths before beginning, or when he looks up and then looks back down at the clipboard. I loosen the fingers wrapped around my wrist, feeling a little lighter. The possibility of having lost more, of having the control when they were trying so hard to wrestle it back, almost made me smile.

Dr. M says, "At this point, I think we need to strongly consider inpatient therapy."

I translate in my head. *Wes is too thin, you're not forcing enough food down his throat.*

Mom asks, "Is he doing any better?"

*How guilty should I feel?*

Dr. M replies, "It's quite common for patients like Wes to struggle to heal. Especially when they stay in the same environment where they initially developed the condition."

*Eh, I mean there's a chance you contributed to the whole thing and didn't really fix it. But you can tell yourself it happens to other people, too.*

This goes on for some time, both skirting around Blame and Facts and numbers like Weight and BMI and Cost. It sounds like I'm about to become a balloon person. Swollen, cramping, and fat, and who knows what else.

I start putting on my jeans.

"Wes," Mom says, the way she says full names. The stress building as the word goes on, building tension and subtext and disappointment.

"What? Sounds like I'm going to inpatient, so we're done here."

"Honey, there's still a lot we don't know."

"Oh yeah? Like how I feel about the whole thing? How about how I feel ever?"

I grab my shirt and duck out into the hallway, even though the nurses are all staring at me and everyone is quiet and I can imagine a thousand different things they could be thinking, none of them positive. I wish I had softened the end of each sentence instead of carving them to sharp points, hating how irritable the hunger makes me.

It's only when I get to the parking lot that I realize we drove together. I sit on the curb and don't even bother to pull the fraying sweatshirt over my head. I watch receipts and envelopes tumble across the pavement and float away.

# 46
# BEFORE

"Cails, don't," Mrs. Brennan warned.

I sat down on the stairs facing the front door, pulling my knees up toward me. Footsteps, soft barefoot ones, grew louder, along with the whisper of dragging cloth.

Caila stepped through the doorway, the blanket pulled over her shoulders and hanging behind her. A sad, crochet cape. Her skin was transparent, the color and life siphoned out. Lips, a hypothermic blue. Sunken skin. Eyes weighed down by everything.

She sat next to me, pulling the blanket tighter around her. "I'm sorry." Her head rested on my shoulder and I tried not to stiffen, but she pulled back anyway.

"You know this isn't something I enjoy living with, right?"

"What?" I countered.

"The thoughts. Feelings." Caila picked at a loose thread. "I'm sorry you don't understand, but I'm glad you haven't had to feel how shitty this is."

"As shitty as losing my brother and you in the same day?" It was supposed to be cutting, but my voice cracked, giving me away, and I had to press my hands against my eyes to hold the tears there and even more so when her bony arm wrapped around me.

"I'm sorry." Caila whispered it over and over into my shoulder.

"Are you getting help?" I rested my chin on her head, pulling her closer so I could feel her heartbeat against my skin.

"Yeah, don't worry about me."

"It's my job to."

"That's your only job?" Caila smirked.

"Hmm, well I can also do this." I kissed her forehead, then her cheek.

Caila looked down at her lips then up at me. I started to lean into the electricity between us, the longing in my stomach. She, however, pressed her index finger to my lips, stopping me.

"I'm not that easy." Her smirk grew. I tickled her, eliciting peels of laughter until she kissed me back, her face and lips finally a human shade of blush.

I breathed into her hair for a few moments. "What can I do?"

"Just this—don't walk on eggshells around me. Ask me what you want to know. Remind me of the good things."

"Please don't let me lose you."

"I'm trying."

"Okay." I ran my fingers over her shoulder, brushing my thumb along her arm.

Caila looked up at me, the steadiness of her eyes wavering for once. "You know I couldn't do this without you, right?"

"You could, you're stronger than you think."

Caila rolled her eyes. "You sound like my therapist."

Mom's phone rang in the other room. I stood and leaned on the doorway as she "uh-huh"ed and agreed and hung up. "We need to head down to the station."

"Police station?" I clarified. She nodded. "Why?"

"They didn't say."

Mr. and Mrs. Brennan held each other as we walked out the door, Caila still curled up on the steps, mustering an almost full-sized smile. "Bye."

"Bye. See you soon." I replied, a command as much as a formality.

I plastered on a smile of my own, especially as Mom and Dad looked back at me, their eyes adrift in the sea of unfamiliarity and fear. I was glad when they looked away as my throat tightened and my eyes twitched and dammit I could lose this girl. I had lost Jason. I had to turn back to remember their house was a brown split-level.

Had to tell myself to pay attention to the colors of the shutters on the blur of houses we passed on the way to the station. Decaying tan, sagging eggshell, formerly-baby blue. I squeezed my eyes closed, letting the sunlight and the shadows from trees stretching over the road color the light dancing on my eyelids with strokes of purple and blush and black. Hating that I didn't care about dilapidated houses. Hating that I wanted to care about them and stop caring about things that kept leaving me empty. I was a tea kettle, wanting to be set ablaze with passion and happiness, only to find the fire extinguished and the contents evaporated.

# 47
# AFTER

Mom does not talk the whole ride home. Does not make eye contact, just clenches her jaw and the steering wheel and turns up the soft rock and aggressively hits the turn signal when necessary. She brakes hard so the seatbelt bites into my neck.

Dad is washing dishes and humming, like he used to when Jason and I were little, as Mom throws her shoes to the floor with a thud and runs up the stairs. Dad turns off the water, raising his eyebrow at me for an explanation. I just shrug and make my way toward the stairs.

"How was it?" Dad asks, mid-hum.

I let out a sound that falls between a mumble and a groan.

He sets a plate in the drying rack and turns to face me. "That good? Wow, a miracle."

I start to make my way back to the door, feeling the suffocation of his smile and the positivity hanging around him.

"Guess what?" There's an uncharacteristic excitement to his words.

"What?"

The water turns on, drowning out the chirping birds outside the window. "Never mind, I'll wait until you're in a better mood."

I truly am crazy. A destructive force. The first time I've seen him excited, maybe even happy, and I deflate it with one word. He retreats to the basement.

I run outside, maybe for the freedom, maybe for the fresh air, maybe because I don't know where else to go. The trash cans are lined up obediently at the curb, reminding me of the looping "Wes" envelope and the fact I haven't heard from Caila and she's maybe the only one who will understand. I break into a jog, but the cans are empty and the envelope gone forever.

I run faster, down the street and out of the neighborhood, past patchy, brown lawns and dogs chasing tennis balls and kids laughing on swing sets. The sounds reach my ears distorted, as if I'm underwater. The ground is rolling and unsteady and the sun is too bright and I feel one-thousand pounds and nothing all at once and I can't breathe so I stop and sit down on the curb and hug my fat toothpick legs to myself and wish I had eaten after Dr. M's so I didn't feel so hollow.

I can't go to inpatient. I'm drifting off too much already, barely tethered to earth. Any more food and I'll float away or pop and—what is wrong with me, why can't I just eat?

My stomach growls, pulling me back to the unsteady curb. I taste the metallic cracks on my lips, the dryness of my tongue, the looseness of my stomach.

I slowly stand up despite the protest from my muscles. I stumble down the street until I get to the brown split level. But there's a sign out front. SOLD. And the lights are off and there's no car in the driveway.

I ring the doorbell. It echoes mockingly. I peer inside the window and see nothing but walls. No couch, no chairs, no anything. Caila is gone.

The house starts to blur, the floor undulating. My tongue tingles as everything fades and I feel myself falling.

I wake to the sound of sirens and a tongue on my cheek. Where am I? I open my eyes to a golden puff of a dog licking me. The sky is aggressively blue, but why am I laying under it? I look in front of me, where an elderly lady with a cloud of white hair and fuchsia glasses walks toward the ambulance as it pulls up and two guys jump out.

I start to sit up, despite the pain and the dizziness that try to pull me back to unconsciousness.

"Don't move." The EMTs crouch over me, a hand on my forehead to keep it secured to the earth. They're both slightly taller than I am. The shorter of the two is stockier and red-headed and covered in freckles but with pronounced muscles and jaw bones. The other has dark hair and a close-trimmed beard and piercing blue eyes that take in every bone and fat cell on my body, scanning for injuries, finding inferiority.

I struggle against their callused hands. "I don't need to go to the hospital. I'm fine."

The red head points a light in my eyes. "Pupils equal and responsive."

"What's your name?" the bearded one asks.

"Uh, Wes." It falls off my tongue even though my head feels fuzzy. "Wes McCoy."

"Any allergies?"

"No."

"Little pinch here." Redhead stabs me with a needle at my elbow crease. He secures it with tape. "I'm just getting an IV started to combat the dehydration."

I close my eyes. The sun is too hot and too bright and I feel sick again and the ground is no longer feeling as steady and I know we don't have the money for me to go into this ambulance, especially since we didn't even have money for outpatient or therapy or Jason's funeral or anything.

"Okay Wes, we're going to take you in to get a head CT and to assess why you passed out."

"No," I whisper. Have to clear my throat and try again. "No."

The dark-haired EMT stops. "What do you mean 'no'? You could have a concussion or brain hemorrhage."

"I mean no. I don't want to go to the hospital. I'm refusing care." I feel the earth slip a little beneath me and the edges of my vision go fuzzy. I need to stay conscious or they can take me anyway. Come on Wes.

"Are you sure? It looks like there's something really wrong."

"I'm sure. I'll call my parents."

"Alright," Redhead says. "If you're sure." He begins packing up the ambulance again as the other holds the IV bag and sits next to me, handing me my phone that must have tumbled out of my pocket.

I take it with shaking fingers. They're going to kill me.

# 48
# BEFORE

The police station was hands-down the ugliest building I had ever seen. Comprised of faded brick and warped, cracking concrete broken up only by tiny windows and black-brown trim. An officer approached us as we filed through the door. His body was stuck in-between: between skinny and fat, attractive and not, bearded and clean-shaven, brunette and blond, tall and short. Besides the uniform, he was aggressively average in every respect.

"Mr. and Mrs. McCoy?" he confirmed.

My parents nodded. Mom's hands shook. Dad pulled on the ends of his jacket.

I focused on the corner of orange laminate peeling next to my toe, running my shoe over the edge so it smoothed and popped up again, smoothed and popped up. I wondered why anyone would choose orange for the flooring, much less underneath formerly white rugs for the entrance.

"Officer Ader. Follow me, please." He unlocked a door to the side with his badge and led us past interrogation rooms and rows of cubicles. *Perhaps a cube of cubicles*, I thought to myself. We stopped outside a wooden door with *Ader* inscribed on the brass plaque in the middle. He unlocked it and gestured for us to enter.

The desk that took up most of the space was made from dark cherry and faced the door with three chairs in front. Bookshelves lined the three non-door walls and overflowed with literature and gadgets and certificates.

Mom and Dad sat down across from Officer Ader and I sat next to Dad and wondered where all the oxygen was in the room. I pressed my thumb to my wrist to make sure my heart was still beating and wrapped my remaining fingers around like a bracelet. I twisted the hand around and around after confirming I did, indeed, have a pulse.

Officer Ader clasped his hands together. "We have news about the investigation into Jason McCoy's accident."

"Accident?" I challenged. Death. Say death.

"Wes," Mom warned, flipping to a smile as she turned back to Ader. "Please go on."

"So, after measuring tire tracks we determined Jason was going about seventy-five miles-per-hour at the time of impact."

I bit my lip, trying not to imagine all the things I was imagining.

"We also determined the brakes were not applied and, from witnesses, there was ample time to avoid the truck. Not only was this not attempted but the car actually turned into the semi."

"What are you saying?" Dad had all his muscles tensed. "Surely he was trying to avoid it by going the other direction."

"He was in the fast lane," I said, barely a whisper.

Mom and Dad stared blankly at me.

"If he turned into the semi he turned toward the other lane of oncoming traffic. Toward the concrete barrier it crossed," I said. "He wasn't trying to avoid anything."

"Yes," Ader confirmed. "I'm so sorry, but we believe this could have been a suicide."

"Suicide?" Mom shrieked, standing up so fast her chair thudded to the ground behind her.

No, no, no, no, no. This could not be happening. It was an accident. A death, but an accident. He would never do anything like that. On the way to State? With a full ride? Without saying goodbye?

Dad stood and held Mom, restraining her as she sobbed.

"I'm sorry," Ader said again, as if to the air.

"So, what now?" I asked as I checked for a pulse again. Surely there was none. Surely this wasn't real. But I could feel the heat and the pressure as I twisted my fingers around my wrist and I could feel the pulses jumping against the skin.

Mom's sobs quieted slightly. Dad was crying into her hair now. So why did I feel so numb?

"We are dropping the charges against the driver and at this point stopping the investigation."

"So we'll never know for sure?" My voice cracked.

"I'm sorry." Ader took his hands off the desk, lowering his gaze to a picture frame whose contents I couldn't see from my chair. Probably an aggressively average woman with two-point-five aggressively average children. A dog. None of whom would ever have to sit in an office like this, have to keep saying goodbye to someone who was never supposed to go in the first place. I wondered what Jason would think if he were here. What he would have said if he had left a note.

# 49
# AFTER

"Hello?" Mom has her fake voice on, the one normally reserved for telemarketers and store employees. It's high and permanently agreeable and especially entertaining when it comes with the choice words when scammers call. But it's also her I'm-painting-or-doing-something-else-so-I'm-not-fully-paying-attention voice. Or her I'm-mad-as-hell-right-now voice.

"Mom, I fainted."

"What do you mean?" The fakeness drops.

"I went to Caila's and it's hot out so I fainted, oh and the Brennans are gone and I don't know where she could be, but someone called the EMTs—but don't worry I told them I don't need to go to the hospital—but yeah, Dad didn't pick up the phone, and I need one of you to come get me so they can leave and I'm so sorry I don't know what happened. I don't know what's happening to me and I wish I could make it stop but I can't—"

"Wes," Mom pauses. "Take a deep breath."

"Okay." It's all I can manage to say.

"You're alright."

"Okay." I look up at the hot sun.

"We're coming to get you, we'll be right there."

"Okay." Don't cry. Don't cry.

"You're going to be okay, I promise."

The tears come anyway.

By the time they get to me, I'm able to sit up. The EMTs have packed everything back into the ambulance and Redhead talks to my parents while Dark-hair sits with me. The silence feels heavy, but I'm glad he doesn't try to talk over it. With his help I stand and make my way to the front seat of the car. He closes the door and waves goodbye and I wonder what would have happened if I hadn't thrown away Caila's letter or if I had more water this morning or had walked instead of run or if no one had called 9-1-1. Dr. Simmons would say this was "irrational" or "maladaptive" to believe that I have "control over such things." I believe it's the most rational thing to think of all the things you could have done differently, so you don't keep making the same mistakes over and over and over.

I guess maybe the problem is I'm not good at either.

"Are you alright?" Dad asks as he slides in the back. I nod.

Mom gets in the driver's seat. "I'm glad you're okay."

We drive past the turn toward home but neither Mom nor Dad say anything. There's only the faint whine of the radio, too quiet to hear the words or melodies, but loud enough to be like an incessant mosquito. A minute passes. Then two, then three. My heart is panicking. The buzzing seems more persistent. A bead of sweat forms and rolls down my back.

"Where are we going?" I form my lips around the words, finally forcing them out.

"To get help," Mom says.

I use the silent pause to shut off the radio completely, not daring to probe further.

We cross the bridge into downtown St. Paul. The Mississippi is flowing aggressively, frothing and gushing underneath a glass-blue sky. Mom pulls up to an unassuming building. The majority of the outside is tinted glass and there are no signs to give it away.

"Okay, I'll park the car and meet you inside."

Dad comes around to my door. I let him help me up and take my arm as we shuffle into the lobby. A greeter's desk faces us, but is vacant, as are the clusters of chairs to the sides. On the wall is a directory, but it is stuffed full of acronyms and numbers and my brain is already having enough trouble processing Life.

Mom joins us and we make our way to the elevator and no one is saying anything, or even breathing irregularly, and I wonder if I should make a run for it, even in my weakened state. With a ding, the elevator doors close ominously. I can practically hear the Jaws theme song crescendo-ing in the background.

My stomach growls, perhaps for comedic relief. No one laughs. I close my eyes for a second, imagining ice cream melting on my tongue, the euphoria of sugar, of milky calories. Just thinking about it makes me feel calmer. The doors finally open to a large poster of a girl, her blonde hair in ringlets, holding an overly-bright sunflower. Uh oh, this was not a good sign. Sunflower Center. Making the world a better place for one child at a time.

This seems to promise the kind of nurses who only speak in affirmations. *Happiness is beautiful,* they say as they jam you with needles. *Isn't today a great day to be alive?* as they pat your back while you vomit up bile.

The waiting room looks like a standard doctor's office. Tan walls, dark patterned carpeting, clusters of semi-comfortable chairs, fake plants, *Health* and *Car and Driver* and *National Geographic* strewn on side tables. There is only one other family there, a mother with thick, blonde streaks in her brown hair and a girl around thirteen, all glasses and braces and dark hair popping out of a French braid. A woman at the front desk looks up with a smile that compliments her bright pink scrubs. *Lauryn,* according to her badge.

"Hello!" She seems to speak in overly-happy exclamations. "What can I do for you?"

Mom steps forward. "Wes McCoy to see Dr. Renato."

"Okay, great! I'll check you in and you can have a seat! Someone will call you back shortly!"

Dad pulls out his phone, holding it away from his face and squinting at the screen as he scrolls through email. Mom flips through *Health,* but her eyes aren't focusing. The girl across from us starts to suck on a piece of hair that has escaped the braid, closing her eyes as saliva coats it into a point. The mother looks up, angrily pulling it out of the salivating mouth and tucking it behind a tiny ear. The strand promptly falls back into the girl's face.

"Wes?" Another pink-scrubbed nurse steps into the waiting room, looking up from a clipboard. All three of us start to get up. "Just Wes for right now."

I follow her, down the hall, past exam rooms wafting of disinfectant and nurses' stations buzzing with phones and chatter and the slipping of papers through fingers. "Alright, hon." She leads me into an office labeled *Renato, MD* and the door closes and I'm sure there has been some kind of mistake.

# 50

# BEFORE

When I got home from the police station I went straight to Jason's room. I felt like I could breathe a little more. I picked up the stack of papers on the floor. Receipt. Math assignment. Wrestling schedule. Magazine. More assignments. Ugh. I threw them back into the corner, ripping books off shelves. Calculus textbook, *Romeo and Juliet*, a Spanish novel, a cheat book for Super Mario.

There had to be something. A clue, a reason.

None of his jeans or sweatshirts had anything in the pockets, besides a total of thirty-seven cents, a crumpled index card with smeared physics equations, and a stick of peppermint gum.

I unzipped his backpack and waded through crumpled tests and papers, notebooks and pens. Tucked in between the yellow Physics folder and the blue Spanish folder was a red file. Stanford.

I opened to the first page where a group of students of various ethnicities and genders have their arms around each other as they're perched on a stone wall. All smiling radiantly. Happy to have picked the Perfect University so all their Dreams could Come True.

I flipped to the next page which listed the majors and minors. Theatre arts. Studio arts. Art history. Architectural design. Art practice. Capstone in the arts. CS and art practice. Flipped to the next page, which showcased a collage of rustic buildings, trees blooming in fall colors, more kids laughing and learning.

The next page was a collage of stats: 16,430 students, 7,062 undergraduates, 8,180 acres, 40 academic departments, 117 NCAA team championships, 512 NCAA individual championships, 270 Olympic medals (139 gold), 81 Nobel laureates, 27 Turing laureates,

8 Fields medalists. Alma mater of 30 living billionaires and 17 astronauts.

I was mesmerized. By the numbers and the letters in flowing script in front of a watercolor background. I could see why Jason was in love with this school.

On the next page was the school motto and I had to set the booklet down and look up at the ceiling after I read it, the lights blurring. *Die Luft der Freiheit weht.* The wind of freedom blows.

Jason was supposed to be there, free, getting out of this house and this city and this life.

But on the next page I froze. Average ACT. SAT. GPA. Three letter acronyms that were four letter words to me. A yellow post-it sat in the corner of the page.

> *$58,900 x4= $235,600 total cost. Potential need-based aid-$50,000? ← $42,000 scholarships and $8,000 loans/campus employment. $8,900 not covered if no wrestling scholarship.*

I closed the booklet and threw it on the bed. I pressed my palms to my eyes, sighing. Why couldn't he be the kind of person to hide *Playboy* instead? I rolled my eyes—at least that would be useful.

My phone buzzed. Caila: *Hey, everything okay?*

I put the phone down, curled up around myself in the middle of the room, hand clenched around a tuft of carpet. How did he get off free and we get left with all the heaviness, multiplied? The hollowness, hollowed farther by the lack of him? Did he think of us, care that we would feel this way? Probably, right? Then why go through with it? Why not ask us for help?

My phone buzzed again. I turned it off and closed my eyes.

# 51
# AFTER

Dr. Renato is not the white-haired, balding man I was expecting. He looks barely old enough to be out of school and has an enviable amount of muscle and thick brown hair. The chair spins and he has his feet up on the desk, arms behind his head, mouth formed in a perfect-toothed grin.

"Wes! My man. Good to meet you."

"Uh, hi." I stuff my hands into my pockets and the door closes behind me.

"Come on in, have a seat."

I sit. The chair is comfy, almost like memory foam. I need to find something not to like about this guy. I scan the books behind him—mostly psychology. The decor is fairly understated, except for the *Starvation* poster. Oh, and the Beatles albums. Damn, who was this guy?

His eyes follow my gaze. "You play *Starvation*?"

"Yeah."

"The video game, I mean, not just in life?" He's teasing me?

I can't help but laugh. "True, I do both."

He takes his feet off the desk, leaning forward slightly, eyes hardening. "Important question."

I swallow.

He lets out a smile. "Who's your favorite character?"

Whoa, he's not going to jump into repressed traumas and such right away? "Definitely Kenta."

"Oh, yeah, Kenta's solid." He nods. "I'd have to go with Basir though. Way better tools."

"Okay, but who cares about tools when you barely have any strength to survive?"

"Sounds like you just don't know how to use tools."

I shrug. "Sounds like you just don't know how to play the game."

Dr. Renato laughs. "So here's the deal, Wes. How fast you get better and get out of here is up to you. I know you're smart enough to realize we're just here to help you."

I nod.

"We'll meet every day for the first few days. I'll also schedule you with a nutritionist, group, and possibly a psychiatrist if needed."

"What's group?" I sink into my seat. Maybe this won't be so bad.

"You and other patients meet together. Talk through issues, gossip, ya know?"

I try not to smile, I really do.

"So, I'm going to talk to your parents while Jolene brings you back to your room. *Capiche?*"

"Capash."

Jolene, the same woman who brought me to Dr. Renato's office, has a high, blonde-ponytail and an excess of makeup and wrinkles, but the kind that come from smiling too much. "Hi hon. How are we?"

I smile at the Collin-ism. "Okay, thanks. You?"

"Great, hon. So dinner is soon. If you eat everything on your plate in the time period, you get a point. An extra for drinking your replacement shake."

"It's worth it, man," a deep voice booms from the room ahead of us. "Might not seem like it, but worth, fo' shizzle."

I turn to Jolene. "Who's that?"

"Your roommate, Alex Mason, hon."

I lean in the doorway. Alex lays on his bed, red Beats around his neck. The walls over his bed are peeling but there's a crooked picture of a girl in lingerie taped in the middle. Jolene rolls her eyes and pulls it down.

"Babe, how many times do I have to tell you?"

"What did you mean, 'worth it'?" I ask, circling back to Alex's previous comment.

"Oh, man, first of all, those shakes are the bomb. Chocolate velvet fo' sho'." He sits up. "Plus leveling up? Tomorrow I can go to the movies for the first time in forever, my man. Living the damn dream."

Leveling up? And who was this kid? He talks like this and looks like he was plucked straight from a very average suburban house with a mother who loves Tupperware as much as spin class.

A bell tolls, static-y, over the PA system.

"Can you take him to dinner, hon?" Jolene asks Alex. She hands me the same T-shirt Alex is wearing of a sunflower, along with gym shorts. "And put these on, please, babe."

"Def." Alex head-nods an acknowledgement.

I haven't even been here thirty minutes and already they're starting to try to fatten me up.

# 52
# BEFORE

When I woke up, everything was grainy with darkness. The imprint of Jason's carpet had etched onto my face and my stomach let out a growl. I tiptoed downstairs, stopping at the bottom as the kitchen light flicked on. A cabinet door thudded closed. Glasses tinkled, hitting each other. I peeked in. Mom slouched over the table, her back to me, hands gripping a steaming cup of tea. The tie of her baby blue robe hung limply, brushing against the worn hardwood.

I took a step forward, but the floor creaked beneath me, breaking the silence with a squeak. Mom jerked upright.

"Oh, it's you." She brushed her hands over her cheeks, hastily.

"Couldn't sleep?"

Mom shook her head, biting her lip to try to keep the tears back.

I stood behind her and wrapped my arms around her, a semi-awkward half-standing/half-sitting hug, but she wrapped her arms around mine, pulling me closer.

I thought about Collin in the hallway yesterday, before I was swallowed up by shoulders and people, of the way we will talk about wrestling from now on. Never saying his name because that would make it real. Saying, "Yeah, he was good, wasn't he?" *Yeah. Feels weird without him, doesn't it?* "Yeah."

And it was such an un-Collin-like thing to say, *yeah*, but there will be nothing else to say besides *it sucks* or *he's in a better place* or a million other things that say nothing about how shitty it was to lose him, and all I wanted was for Collin to make some joke and for me to laugh and not feel like my heart was missing or broken or infected.

And then there was Caila. Who I could understand completely and not at all. Who I needed to get better so I didn't lose her as well, and who I needed to lose before losing her hurt too damn much.

"Wes?" Mom whispered into my arms, still holding on tight.

"Yeah, Mom?"

"I love you, you know that?"

I nodded, holding her tighter.

After a few minutes I handed her a tissue and washed my face in the kitchen sink, even though it meant I had to use the scratchy, yellow towel.

"Do you want something to eat?" Mom stood in front of the stainless steel fridge.

"Like what?"

"Oh, I don't know." She opened the doors then turned the kettle on for more tea before turning toward me. "Eggs, sausage, sandwich, milk, yogurt, fruit?"

I laughed. "Yeah, I'll eat some milk."

She rolled her eyes, getting out a glass.

I noticed water by the sink, either from a broken pipe or from me or a combination, but right as I took a step forward to clean it up, Mom stepped in it, sending the glass flying as she fell to the floor. The boom and crash echoed through the house.

For a second everything was silent. Then, she started to giggle. Carefree and high-pitched with a snort or two thrown in for good measure and I couldn't help but laugh along.

Footsteps thudded behind us. "What the hell is going on?"

I swallowed my smile. "Nothing, Dad. Mom just fell."

"For Pete's sake. Some of us are trying to sleep."

I said nothing, grabbed the broom and began to sweep.

"Are you deaf or just dumb? At least let me know you heard me."

I bit my lip, gripping the broom until it cut into my palms. "I heard you."

Mom stood, her face white. Silent.

I dumped the dustpan in the trash as Mom washed her hands and dried them on the scratchy, yellow towel that left them even redder than before.

"Goodnight," I whispered, retreating up the stairs.

"Goodnight."

On the way back to my room, I ducked into Jason's room because the door was still open. The darkness seeped into the hallway, along with the cold from outside. I flicked on the light, the Stanford folder having fallen, scattering paper everywhere.

I picked up the pieces, stopping as I grabbed the last sheet. One I hadn't seen the night before. A list of schools—Stanford, at the top, but underneath were Minnesota, Rice, Bowdoin, Swarthmore, UChicago, Wisconsin. Harvard was crossed out, as was Colombia. There were arrows off of each. In-state tuition came off Minnesota and Wisconsin. Architecture—Wes—was pointing to Rice.

I flipped over the paper, where Jason had written bullet-points. Top architecture program. Art minor or double major? Scholarships and financial aid $$.

No, I couldn't go to Texas. I couldn't get into a selective architecture program. I hadn't ever designed a building, nonetheless one that could stand. Nope. I could work at Blick supplies my whole life. Go to the bar and reminisce about the Good Old Days with Collin and Nate and Andre until we only talked about our back pain and politics. Live with Mom and Dad, maybe move to the basement, until they kicked me out or I turned thirty-five or got married or whatnot.

Sorry, Jason. We couldn't all be like you.

# 53
## AFTER

The cafeteria is about as stereotypical as cafeterias can get. Long, wooden tables in rows. Grumpy looking ladies in hairnets. Clumps of kids, clustered together. Cartons of milk and bowls of fruit of questionable quality. Large trash cans at the entrance and plastic trays and boards above the lines proclaiming *Tasty Tacos* and *Burgers and More*.

The kids, however, do not fit the stereotype. They all wear yellow T-shirts and black gym shorts. Some have hospital socks with the white grips on both sides, some just tennis shoes. A cluster of girls, comprised solely of protruding bones and thin, feathery skin and straightened-to-death blonde hair, sit near the door, cackling. Behind them, a group of girls as overweight as the others are thin trade quesadillas under the table until a nurse approaches and reprimands them.

On the same wall as the entrance door, a large monitor projects initials and two numbers. The first ranges from one to four while the other extends into double digits.

"What's that?" I point.

Alex starts leading me through the rows of tables as he talks. "That keeps track of what level everyone is on, ya know? And then how many points to level up."

I make eye contact with multiple people—a small boy in glasses, holding a half-eaten apple, a college-aged girl with braces and a scowl, girls who had cut the collar of their shirt into a V, and boys who had cut the sleeves off, and vice versa.

"Okay, you need to explain this whole system. This whole place, even."

"Yeah, it's confusing at first, homie, but it's not that complex once you understand." Alex holds his tray out for some shredded meat sauce substance. "First of all, take a scoop of everything. One meat, one fruit, one vegetable, one bread, one side, and one replacement." He points at the signs that denote what each counts for, with a cartoon image.

I follow him, wishing the staff was worse at scooping overflowing spoonfuls. One pile of meat sauce substance, something that may be pear chunks, corn that is still hard, a quesadilla, and a chocolate Ensure. As we reach the end of the lunch line, Alex holds out his barcoded wristband. A short woman with gray hair pulled tightly into a perfect bun and bushy eyebrows, scans it, and the screen across the hall changes $AM$ 2 14 to $AM$ 2 15. Level 2, almost level 3, impressive.

Alex tells the woman my name, which she writes down and waves us through. We sit down next to the windows, about halfway back, next to people Alex greets with "'sup?" He gestures to the girl next to me. "This is Skye Williams." She raises her hand and gives me a smirk, her black curls bouncing, nose stud glinting.

Alex adds, "Guys this is Wes."

"I'm one of the 'guys' now? Why is a group always referred to in the masculine form?" Skye rolls her eyes at him. "Glad to see the patriarchy is alive and well already today."

"Yep. I, as a bulimic guy, am determined to solidify gender roles in our society," Alex replies sarcastically, shaking his Ensure. Before Skye can retort, he points to the muscular guy across the table. "And this is Dylan Carrera."

"Hey, nice to meet you." Dylan has a dimple beneath the left side of his smile. Besides his expression, everything about him seems hard. Protruding biceps, buzz cut, jaw.

The loudspeaker crackles. "Heeeyy." I can tell even with the static distortion it's Dr. Renato. A few people smile. "Twenty-five minutes," he sing-songs.

I look down at the heaps of meat and quesadilla and too too too much food. Skye leans over. "It tastes better than it looks. And there's less there than you think."

"Thanks." I reply, feeling a little bit of the tension ease. I pick up a forkful of meat and put it in my mouth and it's tender and saucy and oh my gosh this is what food tastes like, no wonder it isn't good for you.

A nurse is positioned next to each table, leaning on the window or wall. Her eyes scan each tray, each mouth.

"Do you guys remember your first Caf meal?" Dylan asks, already halfway through his tray of food. I wonder why he's here, especially since I can't imagine Dylan as anything other than purely muscular.

"Oh, man," Alex shakes his head. "I didn't eat anything the whole first week, remember?"

Skye shrugs. "I don't know about you guys, but it was kind of a relief for me, you know? Like I had to eat what was there, so it wasn't my fault because I just had to."

"Yeah, I feel that," Alex replies, downing his entire Ensure.

"For me it was worse," Dylan says. "Not having that control when that control was all I had left? Brutal."

I wonder why the buzz cut and the muscles are there. He doesn't seem like the kind of person that should be made of hard angles. Unless he needed them, to hold up the mushy inside.

I take a bite of fruit, which I confirm is pears, and almost close my eyes at the sweetness. The soft chunks dissolving in my mouth, filling the hollowness in my throat, my chest, my stomach. Everyone has stopped talking and is looking up at me, a mixture of concern and understanding and apprehension. The bliss explodes and I can't breathe.

"What?" I ask. "As much as I wish purging were a reflex, it's not."

"You never know, honestly," Skye laughs.

"It's just, we've all been there, ya know?" Alex says. I wonder if it is the most empathetic thing he's ever expressed. "Speaking of, how's level three?"

"Oh my gosh," Skye answers. "Literally the best. This morning I got a pass to go downtown. Picture it—waffles. Whipped cream. Strawberries. Real maple syrup. And a protest."

Dylan is practically salivating. "Real maple syrup?"

"You know it. The only thing sweeter than equal rights."

Alex rolls his eyes. "What were you protesting this time, homie?"

"Plastic. Did you know eight million metric tons a year end up in the ocean?"

"Riveting." Alex monotones, at the same time I say, "Wow, really?"

"Wait, so how do levels work exactly?" I take a sip of the Ensure, trying to focus on them and their faces rather than the constricting of my stomach.

"Level one, which is you, bud, means all your meals are supervised in the Caf."

"Two, though," Dylan jumps in. "You can go out every few days, but not at meals."

"And three you can go out, but at meals, too?" I guess.

Skye nods. "Whipped cream and maple syrup, that's all I gotta say."

The loudspeaker crackles. I still have a whole tray of food.

# 54
# BEFORE

I woke up to Mom banging on the door. "Wes, it's six-thirty. Are you up?"

"Uh, yeah Mom." Shoot. I picked up my phone and turned it on as I pulled on jeans. I should've set an alarm. I sat back on the bed when I saw how many texts were on my phone.

Collin: *Hey are you ok?* and *Did you see the news?* and *Are you going to school? I can get your assignments.*

Caila: *What happened?* and *Oh my gosh are you ok?* and *You don't think he did it, do you?*

Nate: *Is it true?*

Andre: *Sorry to hear, man.*

I ran downstairs. "Turn on the TV."

But it was already on and Mom was white and Dad had broken the pencil he was holding as he raked his fork against his plate.

*McCoy Accident Charges Dropped Over Suspected Suicide.*

"I don't feel well," I said, even though no one turned around, and I went back to bed, burying my head in the pillow and pulling the covers over me even when the hot moisture of my breath clung to my skin.

I fell in and out of a restless sleep, waking with a jump, covered in sweat, just as a monster bit through me or I fell to my death or a semi veered off the road and ran into my car. I fished my sketchbook out from under my bed but couldn't bring myself to pick up a pencil, so I dropped it back on the floor and went to the bathroom.

I washed my face, letting the cold water drip as I stared in the mirror. Zombie eyes, all bloodshot and droopy, stared back, the pupils darker than ever. My black hair like tufts of unkempt grass on top of vampire-white skin. The perks of an eternal Minnesota winter.

Jason would have somehow still had a tan. Perfect hair after lying in bed all day. No eye bags, no tear stains—nothing. But now I realized maybe he didn't feel as perfect as he let on. Maybe the permanent smile was as fake as Kathryn's spray tan. I ran a comb through my hair, but it seemed to make the grass-hair stand up even higher, so I snuck downstairs. The lights were off. Dad's car was gone.

My stomach growled, especially as I passed the Costco chocolate muffins on the center island, realizing I had not eaten dinner or breakfast or lunch and it was already 2:30. I got out a plate, white with fading pink flowers on the rim, and ate a muffin in four bites. Chocolatey and moist. I poured a glass of milk and chugged it. Cold and rich and so, so good. I got out strawberries and whipped cream and ate half the carton and finished off the can, the sweetness covering my tongue.

I rummaged around in the fridge, getting out turkey lunch meat and Swiss cheese. Lettuce and mayo and white bread. I made two sandwiches and finished them off, still standing, then polished off the rest of the meat and cheese.

A piece of turkey hung out of my mouth, plates and wrappers covering the countertop, when the doorbell rang. I swallowed, coughing as I choked, sticking my head directly under the tap. It rang again.

Opening the trash can drawer, I swept in as much trash as I could before running to the door and throwing it open. I took a step back, my hand flying to my crazy hair.

Caila stared back at me, head cocked slightly to the side, her hair hanging in damp red ringlets over a Minnesota sweatshirt. She was holding a thermos with a green tea bag swinging from the side. "You didn't answer my texts."

No hello, no nothing.

"Uh, yeah, sorry." I looked down at my bare feet, at the jeans hanging loose where they should have pressed against muscle. *Say you're sorry, too.*

"You could've died or something," Caila said.

I glanced up at her, at the smile playing at the corners of her mouth. "Really?" *Maybe I was right not to text back.* My fingers dug into my palm.

"What? That's the first thing I thought of when you didn't text back last night. Or all of today." Caila crossed her arms, the bones pressing out, but less than they used to.

"Oh yeah, no, it's totally something you should joke about. Not hurtful at all." I crossed my arms, too, leaning into the doorway.

"Seriously? Get over yourself." Caila rolled her green/grey eyes. "If anyone can joke about dying, it's me."

"Why, because you can just decide, at any minute, to be gone forever? And hurt literally everyone around you." I leaned closer. *Geez, how could she continue to be so selfish?*

"You think it's a decision like that? 'Oh, I want to hurt everyone who cares about me now, how do I do that'?" She took a step back, uncrossing her arms. "Eff you."

"Well, clearly if you understood how hard it is to lose someone you would see how stupid it is." I started to close the door, clenching my jaw.

Caila went silent. She unscrewed her thermos. "Yeah, definitely haven't lost my brother, definitely wouldn't know what that's like—"

"Oh, because you could have stopped the cancer, had you known?" I rolled my eyes at her. "Like how I would have stopped Jason has I known? Definitely the same thing."

Caila huffed. "Wow, so I'm not allowed to feel bad about my brother dying?"

"You don't get to know how it feels and then do it to other people!" I yelled.

"Are you saying it's my fault that I was suicidal?"

I shook my head, crossing my arms again. "It's your fault I didn't get to see him again before he gave you his liver!"

She glared at me. "Do you ever ask yourself why he'd rather die than be around you?"

My eyes fixated on her abdomen, right where the scar would be, as my throat tightened. "At least his death could have done some good. Instead of wasting a good liver."

Without missing a beat, she retorted, "At least I'm not wasting my life."

I slapped the tea from her hand, but it splattered all over me instead. The hot liquid landing on my face, gushing down my back, soaking into my shirt and pants and underwear. She dropped the thermos, turning to run down the street, her hair floating behind her, the flame extinguishing as she crossed over the hill. And I just stood there, hot tea dripping down me, collecting into a puddle at my feet, watching her go.

# 55
# AFTER

"Fifteen minutes folks!" Dr. Renato's voice booms from the loudspeaker.

"Time!" Alex says, setting down his fork on a clean tray. The nurse at our window comes and takes it from him, checking his napkin and Ensure bottle before handing it back and allowing him to take it to the tray conveyor near the door.

Everyone else is most of the way done, except me, with two bites gone and millions to go. I force myself to rip off a piece of tortilla and swallow but it's dry and gets stuck and I have to wash it down with Ensure, which actually tastes kind of delicious. I turn it over to look at calories but the nutrition label has been removed. Sneaky.

Alex sits back down, turning to me. "Okay, I'm going to be real with you, homie. You gotta eat faster."

"Oh really? No way!" I retort, stuffing more tortilla in my mouth as I make eye contact.

"Spite eating? Alright, I'll take it."

Somehow, I choke down the whole thing and the Ensure and half my fruit.

"Teeennn minutes, girls, boys, non-binaries, and those that are not sure!"

I'm about to push away my tray and give up for today when my eyes land on Dylan's shirt. And Skye's shirt. And Alex's. All the same yellow sunflower. "Wait, do we get any of our personal belongings?"

"Not really," Skye replies. "Clothes you don't get back until you transition to non-resident. Other stuff like books and activities you can earn back at different levels. I mean, they have books and stuff but not anything worth eating this crap for."

She picks up her fork of meat, letting it splat onto the tray.

"So, like my sketch book? I could get that at level three?"

"Art stuff you can get at level two since it helps you 'cope with emotions'." Skye holds up air quotes.

Okay, McCoy. Now or never. Meat, corn, quesadilla, and the rest of the fruit. It has been forever. I need to draw, to feel the sweet release of pencil on paper, seeing the tangled mess in my brain sort itself out on the paper.

I need to go see Jason, or what's left of him at least.

I need to go see Caila. Make things right with her and what's left of Jason inside her.

I swallow the meat substance in three bites, closing my eyes when my stomach starts to heave, waiting for the waves of nausea and panic to stop. I twist my fingers around my wrist, focusing on the pressure.

Normally, I hate when people comment on my eating. It's like when someone says, "Oh you look tired" or "You've gained some weight, haven't you?" even when it comes in well-meaning comments like "Is that all you're going to eat? Are you sure you aren't hungry?"

But when Alex picks up a fake microphone as the others finish off their dinners, I can't help but laugh. "He could do it folks. Right down to the wire, but he could finish everything! Day one, who would have thought?"

Probably, if anyone else said it, I would have been offended, but Alex is leaning forward, two hands on the invisible microphone, all in on his craft, and I know he knows exactly what I'm going through.

Dylan hands his tray to the nurse. "You know anxiety, especially food anxiety, is reinforced by avoidance behaviors, so eating is one of the best ways to confront it."

"Thank you for those wise words from our very own, Dr. Carrera!"

I almost spit out the last bite of quesadilla with a snort.

"FIVE MINUTES. And counting. Who will prevail?" I can imagine Dr. Renato spinning in his desk chair, holding the intercom.

Pears and corn. My stomach feels like it has been stabbed, but at the same time complete and filled in a way it hasn't in forever. My brain is grinning along with my taste buds, but my throat feels like it has been stuffed with cotton.

"And McCoy stares down the last of the meal, striking fear into its heart. The corn knows this is the end, but McCoy seems to be slowing down."

Skye rolls her eyes as she hands her tray to the nurse. "Don't listen to him. You have like three bites left. You've come all this way. That's like putting capital into wind and solar farms but never plugging them in so they generate energy."

"Or like eating a whole tray of food besides a few bites so you don't get points," Alex counters.

I cram in some corn. You can do this. Finish off the pears. Holy cow I might explode. I put my head down on the table.

"Dude, nausea is temporary. Points are forever," Alex says.

"Three, two, ONE MINUTE!" Dr. Renato booms.

"Although you need the calories, your body has begun starvation syndrome—" Dylan starts.

"Holy cow, Wes. You're stressing me out. Just eat the corn, man." Alex grabs my shoulder.

I shake my head, my stomach is bulging, bloated. I can't.

Skye reaches over, loading up the last of the corn onto my fork. The nurse takes a step closer, watching us.

"Ten, nine, eight—"

I sit up as Skye places the fork right in front of me. I open my mouth, chew.

"Three, two, one—"

Swallow. The nurse takes my tray.

"Hands up, that's it, you're dooonne!"

I drop my head back onto the table.

# 56
# BEFORE

I wiped up the tea and changed out of my clothes into sweatpants and a T-shirt and fell face-first onto my bed. The doorbell rang. I buried my face farther into the comforter despite the pain from the burns from the tea. It rang again.

Nope, not falling for it, no way. I looked outside my window after a few seconds of silence and saw Collin walking away, his Starvation disk in hand. I ran downstairs, but by the time I opened the door, he had already driven away.

I deserved more tea in the face. Plastic cheese wrappers still sat on the far side of the counter. I collected them and put them in the trash, feeling bloated and hollow at the same time, crumpling up napkins to put over the mound in the trash.

Why was I like this? I took my T-shirt off, staring at the bathroom mirror. At the food baby swelling, at the unruly hair and eye bags and the bony arms and legs. I gripped the vanity as the floor dipped below me. Maybe the cheese was bad? Mold I didn't see. Either way I definitely ate too much. There was too much going on.

I kneeled in front of the toilet, closing my eyes. My stomach clenched, but nothing came up. I stuck a finger back into my throat, but I coughed and coughed, my tongue constricting.

I needed to throw up. And I was crying because it was too much and not enough and I needed to get rid of the food that was making me feel this way and I needed everything to go back to the way it was before and I needed Caila and Collin and Jason and what was happening to me? What was going on? Why was I like this? There must be something really wrong, really wrong. This wasn't like me. I couldn't breathe. I was choking, right? Breathe, breathe, breathe. But all I could do was inhale these shallow breaths and the room spun, and my chest tightened and my lungs weren't filling up and oh my gosh maybe I was dying. Why couldn't I breathe? Why was everything spinning and darkening?

I shoved my finger in again, this time as far back as I could, keeping it there as the shudders of heaving started because I couldn't breathe anyway and yellow chunks splattered into the toilet, half-digested, smelling of bile. I sighed in relief as I took a shaky breath. Then another. I wiped my mouth with toilet paper, flushed, and rinsed my mouth out, feeling the bloating subside almost instantly. The floor was stable, my vision back to normal, and I felt like I was floating.

And I was the one to make myself feel like this, feel this good.

Back in my room, I crawled into bed and fell into a deep sleep, curled up in the covers, the fan blowing on me, the curtains blocking out the sun.

# 57
# NOW

Alex and I walk back to our room together. "I'm impressed you ate, man. That was cool."

"I'm impressed you went a week without eating." I focus on the white tile floor, my head still pounding, fuzzy dots forming at the edges of my vision.

"Nah, man, the disordered eating was a lot easier than trying to get better." Alex shrugs. "Hard, yeah, and sucked, but easier."

We open the door, jumping a little as Dr. Renato turns around. "Can I talk to you, Wes?"

I turn toward Alex who is nodding encouragingly. "Uh, yeah."

Dr. Renato leads us into the hallway and toward his office, past pictures of fields and sunsets. The ceiling lights seem all too bright and I wince as he speaks, the volume too loud.

"Soo, how was dinner?"

"Uh—dinner? Dinner was good, I guess. You know?"

He stops when he sees my face. "Are you okay? What's going on?"

"I really don't feel well. I'm super nauseous and dizzy." I blink rapidly, trying to focus on him.

Dr. R nods. "That can happen with refeeding."

"And the lights are really bright. My vision is weird." A good one-fourth of what I can see looks like the static on an unconnected TV.

His voice drops an octave in concern. "Okay, it's okay. Just have a seat." He unclips the walkie-talkie from his belt. "Could I have a nurse outside room thirty-seven?"

I slide down the tan wall, my legs bent, resting my head on my knees, even as bony as they are.

A pink-scrubbed nurse with a high black bun jogs around the corner. She is perfectly proportioned with the right ratio of muscle-to-fat-to-body, a perfect balance between model thinness and bodybuilder strength in a way that looks human and healthy.

"Okay, what's going on?" She kneels in front of me and a wisp of hair falls across her forehead and I think maybe I have died, and she is an angel. "I'm Ashley."

"I feel dizzy and nauseous and my vision is weird and I'm light sensitive. Oh, and my head hurts." I suddenly feel like crying, but I don't know why, and then I want to cry because I don't know why.

Ashley presses a stethoscope to my chest, and I inhale at the coldness against my skin but even the intensity of the sensation can't break through the feeling that I'm floating.

"Okay, lungs and heart sound good." Her pink-polished fingers return the stethoscope to her neck before putting a blood pressure cuff around my arm. "Eighty-five over forty-eight. Hmm that's low. Could be shock."

"He did just eat." Dr. Renato offers. "But the headache and vision have me worried."

"How long have you had the headache?"

"I don't know, a few minutes? It's getting worse though." I want to cover my eyes and hug my knees in and put my head down.

"Do you ever get migraines?" Ashley holds up a flashlight, starting next to my face and moving so it shines in my eye and then switching to the other side.

"No."

"Besides that, the only thing I can think of is a concussion, but you haven't had any head trauma have you?"

I blanch. "Uh, I fainted this morning. I might have hit my head."

"But the headache only just started, right?" Dr. R confirms. I appreciate that he can ask the questions I cannot even think to ask right now.

"I mean, concussion symptoms can take hours to days to appear. Have you ever taken any baseline concussion testing?" Ashley asks.

"Yeah, for wrestling." We took the IMPACT computer test every year, although everyone purposely did worse so if they actually were concussed, it wouldn't keep them from wrestling. Except Jason. And me, because he made me promise I wouldn't because "wrestling is temporary, your brain is forever." Not that it was that convincing coming from the guy going to school to wrestle as much, or maybe even more than, for school itself.

"Alright, let's get you to the infirmary until the nausea gets better." She wraps an arm around me to help me stand. I grab her arm as I get up and it's all muscle, all taught. "No TV, no phone, no screens, no thinking too much, no music, no long conversations."

"Anything he *can* do?" Dr. R takes my other arm. I bite back the urge to tell them my legs are working fine.

"Sleep. Lay down. And I'll have Helen get you some paper so you can color or draw."

"Could I have my sketchpad? It's in with my stuff."

Ashley starts to nod, but Dr. R speaks first. "Not until level two, sorry."

We stop at a door covered in drawings of pills and band aids and ice. There are five cots, each with a curtain suspended from a track in the ceiling. All except one is empty, the floral pattern pulled around the bed, blocking out everything besides the occasional creak of the springs. The lights are low and there is the faint scent of disinfectant and body fluids, like at a nursing home. I set my head down on a thin pillow covered in paper as I lay on the equally paper-covered cot.

Ashley pulls my curtain closed. "I'll contact your trainer and coach to get the baseline and check back in a bit."

"And I'll call your parents," Dr. R adds before they both leave.

I count the tiles in the ceiling and trace the patterns they make, studying the flowers on the cloth and the blank space where there are none.

It's only when I find the space where the two edges don't quite fit together that I see who's in the bed across from me. And she has fiery red hair.

# 58
# NOW

Caila turns away as soon as we make eye contact, but I sit up and pull my curtain back part of the way. "Hey."

"Hey, did you get my letter?" She is trying to look at the floor, but her eyes keep finding mine and I keep finding her freckles and the softness of her expression.

"Uh, yes and no."

She's grinning, a dimple forming on her left cheek. As soon as she does, though, I feel myself stiffen, as if my body is preparing for the stress that comes from being around her. But part of me still wants to run my fingers over it, hold her close and whisper how sorry I am, even if it can't melt a whole year of icy separation. *No. She isn't good for you. You're here because of her.*

"What was in the letter?" I look at her, have to look away.

I can't read her expression because she turns and pulls the sheet over her head and I feel like I have been stabbed. I lay down, dizzy, and let myself fall into a restless sleep where I dream I am eaten by a dragon and spat out again.

"Wes, *psst.*" I sit up to Collin perched on the edge of the bed. "We gotta get you out of here."

He peeks around the corner. "Quick, before she comes back."

I swing my legs to the side, eyebrows knitting together.

"I kid, my good sir. The nurse let me in for visiting hours." He sets paper and crayons on the table next to me. "Only the best coloring implements, of course."

I'm having trouble processing which "she" he was talking about and where I am and everything that's going on.

"Gracious, McCoy, you must have hit your head pretty hard. You are in rehab. Ree-haab."

I roll my eyes at him. "I got that part."

"And there are visiting hours, where kinsfolk and friends may visit."

I sit back in bed, glaring at his pretentiousness, despite my smirk.

"And the hot nurse, Ashley, allowed for me to converse with you here. So as much as I would have liked to converse with her—"

"—and do things other than converse."

"Precisely. I chose to keep my dear friend company instead."

"Wow, you really are a selfless, good Samaritan."

"Indeed. It is hard to be so good in such a world as ours." Collin hangs his head in fake disappointment.

"I wouldn't know."

We both laugh. Collin looks around before opening his bag and pulling out the Starvation disc. "Look what I snuck in."

I hold back another laugh. "Uh, how did you think we were going to play?" I gesture to the electronics-free room. "And, uh, you know I'm concussed, right?"

"Semantics, McCoy."

"That didn't even make sense."

"Sure it did, if you were educated in the English language it would make perfect sense."

"Right. I'm the one with a loose grasp on situational awareness and contextual clues."

Collin clutched his chest. "Why doth thee wound me so?"

He puts the disc back into his bag, setting it on the floor. I roll my eyes. "So, Mom and Dad aren't coming?"

"They're coming later. Talking with the boss dude now about payment, I think."

I groan and pull the pillow over my head.

"What?"

"I forgot about that. We don't have the money for this."

Collin says nothing.

I take the pillow off and he's grinning. "What?"

"I was supposed to wait to tell you with your parents. Well, actually Caila was supposed to tell you until you effed that up."

"Well now you have to tell me." I peer through the curtain gap but Caila's bed is empty.

"Coach and the team and I started a fund, the Jason McCoy Legacy Fund, and we raised money, and will raise money, for Hayfield students to get mental health help."

I stare at him. Really?

But also, his point is?

"And we agreed unanimously to pay for you to go to Sunflower with our first chunk of money."

I hug him. I can imagine Mom and Dad smiling in the light way they hadn't in forever.

"Careful," Collin laughs. "I coiffed my hair this morning."

I give him another hug. "You're the best, you know that?"

"Indeed, I do."

I roll my eyes again.

# 59
# NOW

Collin leaves as my parents walk in cautiously. Mom pats the cot to make sure my legs are out of the way before sitting down. Dad stands behind her, bent slightly, wrinkled slightly.

"Thank you for being here, Wes. I know it's hard." Mom runs her hand over the edge of the sheet.

"We're proud of you," Dad says, resting his hand on Mom's shoulder.

"For what?" I say, letting my hands fall onto my lap.

"For trying to get better, we can't imagine how painful of a process it must be."

"And we're sorry if we contributed to this in any way." Dad's expression shifts. "Besides the faulty genes, of course."

"Yeah, you know, I was just thinking we needed to have a talk about that," I reply sarcastically.

"There is something we should tell you, though," Mom looks back up at Dad. Lightness dances around her face.

"Collin told me about the scholarship," I confess sheepishly.

Dad rolls his eyes, squeezing Mom's shoulder. "I told you he would."

I shake my head slightly. "That's incredible, though, I can't believe they're doing it."

They're both grinning.

"And I'm sorry about all the medical bills and all that—"

"Wes, honey, stop. Don't apologize for being sick." Mom runs her thumb over my wrist. "You're in great hands here, they really know what they're doing."

"And it's a better excuse to skip school than I ever had," Dad adds.

Mom gives him a look, but it is relatively soft.

"So what happens now?" I say. "I stay here until I graduate the program? And then what? I redo Junior year?"

They make eye contact.

"Well, Collin has graciously offered to bring you school materials and the teachers are going to do as much online as possible for you," Mom starts.

"And Dr. R is going to make sure you get your work done," Dad adds.

Mom nods. "So it looks like you'll finish out the year, but if needed you can take classes this summer."

"You seem proud of me having to go to summer school," I joke, smoothing out the top sheet with my free hand.

"Nah, we're just proud of you in general," Dad replies, lightly punching me on the arm and then pulling me into a hug. I maybe hear some sniffles.

"Good thing visiting hours are restricted," I quip as he finally relinquishes his hold on me.

Dad shrugs. "Don't worry, you'll see more of us than you want anyway."

"Oh yeah? Are you going to sneak in?"

"I don't have to. We have visiting hours and family therapy together and I'll call and write letters and wow, you are going to be really sick of us."

I laugh. "As long as you don't send smoke signals, too. That would be too much."

He shrugs. "No guarantees."

"Oh," Mom picks up her purse, pulling out a blue file. "When you are no longer concussed, Dr. R would like you to fill this out."

"So why is he giving it to me now?"

"So you can start to think about the future while you're stuck in the infirmary."

She hands it to me and I open to the first page. *My goals for therapy are...*and *My goals for life after therapy are...*with spaces beneath each. I turn to the back. *Three physical and three non-physical things I like about myself are...*and *Three non-physical things I can work on...*

"Okay, thanks. I'll try to heal extra fast."

Mom rolls her eyes. "Good, do that."

I tuck the folder underneath the bed so just a small corner of blue is sticking out.

She kisses me on the forehead and Dad squeezes my leg and they both leave.

As I close my eyes to go back to sleep, the springs on the bed across from mine creak.

# 60
# NOW

"Hey," I whisper. Silence answers me. "Caila?"

Nothing but the whoosh of the heating ducts.

"Are you awake?"

Still nothing.

"Caila?"

A groan breaks through. "Geez, Wes. Keep it down over there."

I close my eyes to go back to sleep. *No,* I think, *I'm not going to just sit and wait for something to happen.* I stand up and pull back my curtain, despite the loud clamor of metal sliding on metal.

"What do you want?" Caila turns over just enough to make eye contact, her hair spread out around her head, the sheet pulled up to her chin. Her words are the straight-to-the-point Caila-style without the harshness most people add to them. But when she sees me, she hesitates. "I—I didn't—"

"What?" I feel the anger bubble up again.

"I didn't realize things were so bad. With you."

"Wow, thanks." I start to turn around.

"No, Wes. Sorry. I don't know what to say, okay? I messed up. I'm sorry for what I put you through, I didn't mean to. To drag you into this or to make you suffer or any of that."

I close my eyes. I had wanted for so long to hear her say she was sorry.

"I wanted to help—with the letter. I've said so many things I didn't mean."

"I know." I swallow. "Me too."

Caila sits up, pulling her legs toward her and patting the end of the bed for me to sit. Her eyes trace the sunkeness of my cheeks. "I can't believe—I mean, you just look so different."

"So do you." For once, there's a softness to her cheeks. Something besides bone. "You moved?" It's a comment and a question.

"Mom and Dad moved in with Grandpa and Grandma. And I moved in here." She gestures to her stomach. "Well, we did—my liver and I."

I almost smile. A Collin-ism for Jason's liver.

She leans against the wall. "I know there are people who deserved this maybe more than I did. I would give it back if you could have Jason instead, you know?"

I shrug. "Doesn't work like that."

"But I'm trying. I'm really trying this time, Wes. I want to be deserving of it. I want to get better."

"That's great," I say, trying to look away from where the liver must be.

"You have to, too. Try to get better. Like *really* try." Caila holds my gaze until I nod.

"I know. I am. It's just hard." I pull one leg underneath me on the bed, the other dangling above the concrete floor.

"Can I tell you something?" Caila asks.

I look up. "Uh, yeah, sure."

"I really appreciate what you did for me. All of it. I didn't realize at the time, but I do now."

"Thanks."

"I'm trying to not just get better but be a better person." She shrugs, the tail of the scar peeking out of the bottom of her shirt. "I just wanted you to know."

The room is too quiet, even with the constant whoosh of air.

"Hey, can I ask you—I mean I don't want to, like—"

"Wes, just ask." She pulls her shirt down, so I don't get to see the entirety of the angry line.

"Did you leave a note when you took the pills?"

"No." She takes a deep breath. "I tried, I really tried. It's just, what can you say in one note to make people understand? To make them not hurt as much? When I didn't understand fully myself and still don't."

I close my eyes.

"And you know with Jason, he didn't have time to write a note, it was a last minute decision. To do it right then, anyway."

"But he had to have been in a bad place for a long time."

"Yeah." She nods.

"And he probably thought about it before?"

"Yeah."

"But I should have known, shouldn't I?"

"Because he made it obvious, wanting people to know, like you did with your disorder?" she counters.

"But he wasn't like crying all the time. I would have noticed if he was."

"Depression isn't just that, especially with guys. He could have been more irritable or withdrawn or something."

For the first time, things start to make sense.

I thought back to the night before State, how he had yelled at me about the water bottle. How he had said I was lucky for not having to worry all the time. How I only saw him at dinner most days.

"So why then? Why on the way to State?"

"That's the thing about suicide. It isn't rational, but it feels rational at the time."

I pick a lint ball off the bed, rolling it between my fingers. "Thanks, that helps. I mean, I don't think I'll ever fully understand it, but at least I think I understand it better."

"I don't even fully understand it. Just don't think it was your fault, please. I would have hated if people thought it was their fault." Caila places her hand on mine and I give her a smile.

"Thanks."

Caila tips her head back so it's leaning against the wall. "What are you going to do when you get out of here? They keep asking me, but I just don't know."

I take a breath. What am I going to do?

"Have you heard of Rice University?" I ask. "I think I want to go there."

She's smiling.

"What?" I give her a nudge.

"Nothing."

"No, really, what?"

"I just missed you is all."

"Yeah? I missed you, too."

"Do you think we could work? Or at least try to make it work again?"

"I don't know. I don't know that much about you," I say honestly, with a shrug. "I think you're beautiful and smart and brave. And I know I get butterflies around you whenever you let your guard down, like with the snowball fight or our first date."

"Oh yeah?"

I roll my eyes. "Yeah, but I have a lot to work on before I am where I need to be."

She's smiling, leaning forward, her arms no longer clutching tightly to her legs, her posture softens as her eyes trace my face.

"And you have lot to do before you're healthy." Caila nods, so I continue. "I guess I'm saying I want to try to make it work, but I don't know—" and her lips are on mine and I'm thinking about nothing but her. The softness of her lips, the pressure. Her fingertips on my cheek, leaving trails of electricity. Her knee touching my leg, softly at first.

And I hope more than anything to get better. To feel what I'm feeling now, over and over.

With or without her.

THIS ISN'T A LOVE STORY. A fantasy. A fairy tale. But this is my life.

And I don't know how my story ends, and maybe that's part of the beauty of it.

Maybe I get a happy ending. Recover from my eating disorder, even if I will forever have a different relationship with food.

But maybe I won't. Many of us don't, you know. Many of us don't even get to tell our story.

# ACKNOWLEDGMENTS

First of all, thank you to my Immortal Works team for everything you did to make this book what it is. I'm eternally grateful to Rachel Huffmire for taking a chance on me, and being the first to believe in my story. Many thanks to Holli Anderson for being an amazing editor and supporting me through the process. This book wouldn't have been possible without Ashley Literski's creative expertise, Beth Buck's coordination, Staci Olsen's production management, and the help of everyone else on the Immortal Works team.

My parents made sure I grew up surrounded by books, and instilled in me a love of reading and writing. You were there cheering me on at every volleyball game, helping me move every year for school, and being a constant support, for better or worse. Thank you for all of this, in addition to your continued encouragement and love. I also appreciate the rest of my family and all you've done for me—from investing in my education, to telling friends (and anyone who will listen) about my book, to being there through the holidays and heartbreaks.

Thank you to Bella Haake, for being the best friend and beta reader I could want. Your support of me, as a writer and person, means the world. I couldn't have gotten to where I am without you.

To Nasreen Fynewever, who first introduced me to the world of publishing, and helped me through all stages of the process. I appreciate your mentorship and encouragement throughout my publishing journey.

I am indebted to Rachel Pastan for your teaching and advising during my time at Swarthmore College. Your lessons on the craft of writing, from short stories to novels, were crucial in forming who I am as a writer today.

Thank you to the Molly who inspired this book, even if she doesn't know she did. Your kindness and strength are impressive, especially in the face of such a devastating illness. Even though your story isn't portrayed here, the juxtaposition of your hidden struggle and your positive disposition, inspired me to learn more about (and ultimately start a career in) eating disorders.

Additional thanks to everyone who beta-read for me (including Karma Chesnut), my friends for the laughs and love, my coworkers at the Minnesota Center for Eating Disorders Research including Dr. Scott Crow, Dr. Carol Peterson, Dr. Lisa Anderson, and Dr. Annie Haynos (even though this book was written before I knew you, you have already taught and inspired me tremendously).

Finally, to everyone who took the time to read this book: thank you. It means the world to me that you chose to go on this journey with me, and I hope you got as much out of reading this as I got out of writing it.

# ABOUT THE AUTHOR

Molly Fennig studied Neuroscience, Spanish, and English at Swarthmore College. She has published in The Blue Route Literary Magazine, The Blue Nib, the Running Wild Press Anthology, Havik 2020 Anthology, other literary presses, and multiple scientific journals. Molly currently works at the University of Minnesota in eating disorders treatment research and hopes to get her doctorate in clinical psychology.

Outside of her passion for writing and mental health, Molly enjoys eating large quantities of chocolate and spending time with her goldendoodle, Mocha.

Find out more about Molly at her website, mollyfennig.com, or on Twitter (@mollyfennig) or Facebook (mollyfennigauthor).

This has been an
Immortal Production